STOWAWAY

THE ISLAND ESCAPE SERIES

STELLA QUINN

1

Sabrina read the words scrolling over the screen of her phone and felt no emotion. *Registration suspended ... compromised patient safety ... administrative tribunal.* Once, she would not have believed that she, Dr. Sabrina Gray, could be accused of incompetence, or have her skills questioned. But now? Here, a little after midnight, in a booze-and-reggae-fueled bar on the disco strip of an island in the Caribbean, she just didn't care. It had been so long since she'd cared about anything but the nightmares.

"Can we buy you a drink, princess?"

Two young men, hardly more than boys, leaned on her table, the rum on their breath even more offensive than their luridly flowered shirts.

"Get lost, boys."

She turned her head, gazed past them to the dance floor where her friend Antonia had disappeared. She wondered if Antonia would notice if she just slipped away. Bars, music, fun...nothing was fun anymore, not even on the sun-kissed holiday island of Ballena. Not for her.

The drunken youths swung into the empty chairs at her table, sure of their welcome. She shot a dark look in the direction of the bouncer, who was engrossed in chatting up a pretty little blonde thing at the doorway who didn't look old enough to gain entry to anything besides a school prom. He'd be no use, clearly. She gave the table a once-over. The warm dregs of cocktails swam under limp umbrellas and toothpicks of fruit. There was nothing here she needed. She snagged her friend's purse from over the back of the chair where Antonia had slung it with gay abandon almost an hour ago, and resigned herself to fighting her way through the throng of sweaty bodies on the dance floor.

Smoke billowed from the DJ pit, garishly lit by rows of colored lights. She leaned back as a scantily clad torso shimmied towards her, dodged a couple possessed by more energy than rhythm, then spotted her friend.

Thank heaven. Despite her tiredness, despite the fog of apathy that traveled everywhere with her these days, she smiled. Antonia was locked in the arms of the pilot she'd met on her first day here in Ballena. That girl could find a silver lining in a hurricane.

A crash sounded behind her, and she spun. A waitress swooped to the floor to gather up shards of broken glassware and Sabrina shuddered, hurriedly averting her eyes. Not tonight, she told herself, plunging deeper into the crowd. She was too fragile to think about sharp edges and soft skin tonight.

She focused on her friend's face instead. She and Antonia had both run away to the Caribbean. Antonia's love life had come unstuck, for about the third time in a year, and she'd decided the only thing that would soothe her bruised heart was a holiday of sunshine and palm trees.

Sabrina didn't expect anything could soothe her own heart, but she'd jumped at the chance to get away from London, from her mother, from the shattering dreams that woke her from sleep night after night.

Coming to Ballena wasn't a holiday for her, she knew that. She'd run away, absconded, escaped. What she hadn't thought through was what miserable company she would be for her fun-loving friend.

She slipped her way between the last few couples dancing between her and her quarry. Luckily Antonia had found something else to focus on other than Sabrina's misery, and nothing focused her friend's attention more than a strong pair of arms in a well-fitting uniform.

Sabrina had discovered she wasn't receptive to her friend's well-meaning attempts to help, because that would mean acknowledging what the problem was, and how could she possibly do that? She wanted to wallow. She *deserved* to wallow.

She flicked a glance at her watch. Midnight was long gone, and the couple of glasses of wine she had indulged in over dinner had combined with the dance music to cause a throb somewhere behind her left temple. She'd give Antonia her purse, then head back to the hotel.

The couple were so engrossed in each other's company, it took them a while to notice her.

"Ahem," she announced loudly in the vicinity of the one ear of her friend which didn't appear to be surgically attached to the pilot's chest.

Startled brown eyes flew open, and Sabrina raised her eyebrows at her friend. "I'm going," she said loudly over the breathy sounds of the current song. "Here's your purse."

"Wait."

Antonia shouted something unintelligible into the pilot's receptive ear before grabbing Sabrina's arm and dragging her over to the relative quiet of the ladies' restroom.

"Is he gorgeous or what?" Antonia said the second the door swung to behind them.

She looked indulgently into the glowing face of her friend and smiled. "Totally gorgeous."

Antonia gazed dreamily into the mirror while she dabbed at the eyeliner melting beneath her eyes, and Sabrina reached behind her friend to smooth a wild strand of her hair back into its high ponytail. She tried to inject a note of enthusiasm in her voice, to share in Antonia's happiness. "Now you've gone and mussed up your hair snuggling into all that buffness."

"So worth it," Antonia said with a grin.

"I hope you're right."

Antonia quirked an eyebrow at her in the mirror. "Well, that's the difference between you and me, Sabrina. I don't mind being wrong every now and then."

Sabrina looked away from Antonia and inspected her reflection critically in the mirror. Tired blue eyes stared back at her, fringed by a thick black ring of eyelashes. Masses of straight black hair fell to her waist, and even after an evening in the smoky, fetid air of the nightclub, her skin retained its pale hue. The Caribbean sun had done little but color her cheeks.

It was the eyes which haunted her. They'd seen

too much. "We both know just how wrong I can be," she said.

Antonia gripped her hand. "Oh, honey. I wasn't talking about your sister. I was just being frivolous about my dismal track record with men. I'm sorry."

Sabrina blinked and mentally cursed herself. Was she trying to spoil her friend's evening?"

"No. I'm the one who's sorry." She shook her head to clear the despondency which clung to her like a shadow. "I'm tired, I think. You know how it goes. Your defenses are always at their lowest when you're having girl-talk in a nightclub ladies' room at one in the morning."

Antonia grinned, pulled a lipstick out of her purse and applied a generous coat of dark plum. "Well, that's a given," she said.

Sabrina watched her friend in the mirror. Antonia had been her confidante since they were freckled first-graders at school. There was very little she couldn't share with her or her other friend Charlotte. She didn't have to hide how she was feeling. "Hadn't you better get back to your pilot friend before some other tourist whisks him off into the distance, leaving a trail of cocktail umbrellas for you to cry over?"

Antonia smiled complacently. "I don't think so. He and I have plans."

"Plans? What sort of plans? Why am I suddenly

feeling nervous?" she demanded, her eyes widening with mock alarm. Antonia was famous for making reckless decisions. She was as reckless and impulsive as Sabrina was dull and... well, whatever she was now. Hollow?

"Relax, Sabrina. We're just going on a little island-hopping adventure on his plane. A day trip. You don't mind, do you?" Antonia's expression grew anxious. "I know we had planned to have this holiday together, but...this guy is special."

She shook her head. "Of course I don't mind. In fact, you should take a few days, see a bit of the islands." She threw an arm around her friend's shoulder in a quick hug. "You two go and enjoy. I've been thinking I might do that diving course we were looking at. It might take my mind off, well. You know."

Antonia gave her arm a squeeze. "I do know. Let's go find Tyler, and we can walk you back to the hotel."

"I think I can manage a hundred feet on my own."

Antonia flashed her a smile. "Okay, then. I'll see you in a couple of days," she said, smacking a boisterous kiss onto Sabrina's cheek before plunging back through the door to throw herself into her pilot's arms.

Sabrina followed at a more sedate pace, using a tissue to wipe the kiss print from her cheek. She couldn't understand her friend's headlong impulses when it came to the opposite sex. She liked male company, sure. She had male friends, colleagues, but she had yet to meet a man who she felt any great stirring of emotion for.

She shrugged her shoulders. It was probably just her. Perhaps she wasn't capable of passion as intense as Antonia obviously was. And maybe it was for the best. She'd made a mess of her relationship with her sister, a fatal mess. She had no business imagining she could make a success of a relationship with a man.

She pushed her way through the double doors to the esplanade. It was warm outside, despite the lateness of the hour, and the air was sharp with salt from the harbor.

A street cleaning machine was bumping and whirring from curb to gutter, a strobe light on its roof sending a whirlpool of reflection across the glass fronts of cafés and souvenir shops lining the esplanade.

Her breath seized, and she felt the tears rising as she remembered that other night, those other strobe lights flickering, flickering ...

Not here, damn it. A sob caught in her chest, and she broke into a run. When would it end? When would she stop reliving that god-awful night?

Time hadn't helped; months had passed, and she

was getting worse, not better. Running away to the other side of the world hadn't helped; the nightmares had packed their heavy baggage and caught a ride on the plane right beside her.

Running to the hotel room in heels along a poorly lit footpath probably wouldn't help either, but at least she'd escape the ghastly flicker of those lights.

She rounded the corner into the bougainvillea-swathed laneway that marked the entrance to the Jewel of Ballena Marina Resort, and a heartbeat later felt her breath being knocked out of her diaphragm. Her body had smacked into a warm, lean, tall someone who was standing in the shadows of the lane.

2

*S*abrina felt herself falling and threw out her hands to save herself. One hand landed in a thorny twist of bougainvillea stems and she winced. Could anything else go wrong, she thought? She was a disaster on heels this evening.

Her other hand settled on something smooth but warm, and as she steadied herself, she realized she was clutching some stranger's belt buckle. Her eyes shifted from the buckle down to a pair of long, tanned male legs clad in dark shorts.

With a gasp, she snatched her hand back from the metal clasp. "I'm so sorry," she said. "I didn't see you ..."

Her words drifted off as her gaze wandered upwards, over a soft, gray T-shirt tucked into a worn leather belt, over abdomen, diaphragm, pectoral muscles, biceps...a hundred anatomy classes from her student years drip-fed the names of muscle groups into her head as she wrenched her gaze, finally, up to the face above.

"Oh," she breathed.

What a face.

Her cheeks flooded with a rush of heat. She felt the muscles in her stomach turn to water. She finally understood what Antonia had been trying to tell her since the day she'd hit puberty. *Wow*.

The man looked like the kind of guy successful Swiss companies used to sell their diamond-studded, adventure-ready wristwatches: blond in a rugged, I-brush-my-hair-once-a-year kind of way, tall, muscled, and as handsome as ... as ... comparisons failed her.

He had a phone pressed to his ear, and his other hand reached out to help her gain her balance.

She managed a tentative smile. "I'm sorry, I seem to have run into you." Surely that breathy, femme fatale tone was from her short sprint down the street? She gave her reeling senses a firm shake. "I hope you're not hurt."

"Hang on a sec," he said into his phone, then turned his attention to her. He frowned slightly, then seemed to realize she'd asked him a question.

"Hurt?" He looked amazed at the suggestion, then quirked his lips. "I'll live."

"I was running," she blurted out, trying to jog her brain into action. "The lights were umm—" She broke off abruptly. No one needed to hear about her crazy dramas with flashing lights. She realized that the surprise of cannoning into a stranger had totally driven her reaction to the lights out of her head.

He held his hands in the air, indicating his phone, "I really have to get back to this. If you're okay."

His voice was a deep American drawl that poured like molasses from a jar. She wanted to wallow in it for a second longer. It had been so long since she'd felt anything but pain and guilt and grief, but this strange flare of attraction had cut through her dulled senses like a scalpel.

"I'd, er...better get going," she muttered reluctantly.

"Me too." He dropped his gaze to hers and gave her a quick grin, obviously unaware of the effect the flash of dimple in his cheek had on women going through an emotional crisis, then wandered off into the darkness of the street. She heard his voice pouring its molasses into the phone that had reclaimed his attention. "No, just bumped into someone. I haven't seen your jacket or your spare keys ..."

His words grew faint as he disappeared from

view, and she lingered by the hotel entrance, feeling the cloak of despair settle over once more. For a moment, she had let herself hallucinate about being a different woman: a happy one, whose life choices hadn't destroyed everything, who might bump into an attractive man on holiday and, gosh, say hello. Get his number, ask him for a drink, behave like a person instead of an automaton. But she wasn't different, she was herself, Sabrina Gray—former sister, disappointing daughter, suspended surgeon—and she was in no fit state to be in the company of anyone.

She swiped her card against the electronic latch on the gate, aware of a flare of regret. Sleep, she thought. Go to sleep, and this wistful nonsense will have evaporated by morning.

SLEEP PROVED ELUSIVE. She lay in the coolness of her room where the hum of the air conditioner nudged her into a fitful doze. Her sister's white face loomed, ghostlike, in the shadows of her dream.

"Why don't you help me, Sabrina?" the ghost whispered. But there was too much blood, too many cuts in her sister's arms. Sabrina sewed suture after suture into the cold skin of her sister's wrists, but the blood kept coming.

She woke on a ragged gasp for air and blinked in

the darkness, lost for a second as she recalled where she was. A hotel room. The island of Ballena. She gave a groan and collapsed back against the pillows. She looked at her hands, at the tremors which shook them now whenever she thought about sutures. Blood. Surgery.

She turned her face to the digital numbers glowing on the clock. It was past four. Sighing, she rose to her feet. She might as well go for a walk within the safety of the hotel complex and try to clear her head. Fresh air was the only thing that helped, and she'd be safe there. She dragged on the bikini that had been drying over a chair, then threw a cobalt blue beach dress over the top. Maybe she'd take a swim when the sun came up, before the hotel's beach grew too crowded with tourists.

It was not quite five o'clock when she set foot on the marina. Usually busy with holidaymakers and boat crew, it was uncannily quiet at this hour of the morning. And cool, blessedly so. Low wattage bulbs threw circles of light along the floating pontoons, and the gleaming boat hulls lay still in the inky water. Sabrina eased her hair from her neck to enjoy the light breeze and listened to the jangle of wires and ropes beating against tall masts.

The salt air and serenity soothed her nerves, and she strolled down the pontoons, forcing her mind away from her sister and her stalled career. Her thoughts skittered back to the man she had met on the esplanade. She had spent years listening to her friends talk about the physical attraction they experienced when they fell for a man. The drum rolls. The heat. She had thought either they were exaggerating, or she was just insipid: a cooler character not programmed to feel that way. But a split-second encounter with gleaming eyes over a soft gray T-shirt had changed all that.

She smiled to herself in the sudden realization that thinking about her reaction to a total stranger had made her feel something. *Something*. For the first time in months, the fog of misery had lifted. And the something she had felt was want. She had wanted that man. She'd been in his presence for about fifty seconds, but that had been long enough for the burn to start.

Life was a contrary thing. Her career as a surgeon was hanging in tatters, her relationship with her mother was strained to breaking point, her grief for her sister had all but consumed her. But here, half a world away from her problems, she'd discovered she wasn't quite the ice queen she'd always believed herself to be. All it took was the right man to light the match.

She slowed her pace as she wandered along the marina berths, picking her way through the coils of rope that crisscrossed the walkway. The variety of boats moored in the marina was astonishing. Monolithic motor launches hogged the prime positions in the marina at the end of each pontoon, and smaller boats of all shapes and sizes filled the other berths. The yachts looked magnificent. Many of them took tourists out, and she decided to keep an eye out for one offering a dive course for her to do, while Antonia was out of town.

She hadn't spent a great deal of time at sea. Her family was more at home on horseback than on water. The odd cross-channel ferry was the closest she'd been to an ocean voyage. She didn't know the first thing about boats. She ducked under a massive bowsprit, running her hand over the curves and furrows of a mermaid carved into its varnished timber.

A hose sputtered drops of water from an ill-fitting tap, and she took an over-large step to avoid the puddle beneath it, landing in the dim shadows between two marina lamps. A spray of plankton caught her attention, its phosphorescence arcing through the inky water, and she looked up, just as her head thwacked into the dark bowsprit of another luxurious yacht which overhung the walkway.

She had been walking on the edge of the pontoon, where the pale rubber bumper lined the rough concrete, and when she banged her head, it was no glancing blow.

She had a sensation of falling. Black spots swam across her vision, and she flailed her arms as her consciousness began descending into a dark and dreamless fog. Her hands grasped at air as she slumped to the ground and rolled, silently, off the pontoon.

3

*T*he first streaks of light were splintering the sky as Ben Ryan turned the ignition key on the *Silver Girl*. The diesel engines he babied like family pets started up at once, and he allowed himself a small smile of satisfaction. After the delays of the previous month, he was itching to get back to sea. The urgent request from Pablo had come at just the right time: a three-day ocean passage to Anguilla carrying supplies was just what he was in the mood for.

Aided by the blinking neon of the yacht's on-deck navigation equipment, he did a quick safety check. Dawn wasn't far away, and he wanted to be at sea to watch the sun rise. When the trade winds picked up, his sails would be set, and being at the whim of the wind would be a welcome change from the past decade of demands.

He paused briefly and let a hand rest on the steel davits rearing upwards from the stern. Okay, that was one detail that was not quite shipshape. The dinghy was normally stowed up there when he planned to be under sail for a few days, but the electric winch had thrown a claw, as his mechanic would say, and was inoperable. He'd tow the dinghy on a long rope, and have a crack at fixing the winch later on that day when he'd switched the helm over to the autopilot.

He flicked a quick glance over the prow of *Silver Girl*. The dinghy was a dark shadow, its blue canopy barely visible. He'd leave it where it was while he reversed out of the marina berth, and then bring it around to one of the stern cleats once he was clear.

He enjoyed the challenge of sailing his yacht single-handedly. Using muscle to set the sails, using his hands on the wheel to adjust the cut of the rudder through the ocean swell...the contrast between the physical exertion of sailing to the mental exertion of computer programming could not be more extreme. It cleared his head. Programming was a world of minutiae, of if-then algorithms which were absolute. Sailing was filled with variables he could not control. And he loved it. The vagaries of the wind, the currents. Sure, he could analyze them, use forecasting and tide charts and maps to his advantage to sail where he wanted to go. But the ocean was dynamic, ever-changing, a challenge that could never truly be mastered.

Freedom. He supposed that was the lure of the ocean, of sailing. And that was why acquiring the neglected timber sloop *Silver Girl* from a San Francisco boat yard had been his first impulsive move when he sold his business, when he was free of the administrative burden that running his internet empire had become.

His ex-girlfriend hadn't viewed the run-down yacht with the same air of optimism. She'd cashed in the chunk of stock options in his company he'd given her and run off to live in a high-rise condo in the heart of New York with some smooth-talking stockbroker who looked like he didn't own any clothes other than suits.

Ben grinned, ran a hand over his stubble, looked down at his bare chest, the tatty drill shorts he wore. This was his idea of work attire now, and he loved it.

He pushed thoughts of his money-loving ex out of his head. That was the trouble with flying Stateside for a few weeks to see his dad, check in with his financial team, make sure his house was still standing. It stirred up memories, ones he could do without.

The *Silver Girl* was the only woman in his life now. And she shone, her brass fittings polished by him, her hull blindingly white, her sails and interior brand-spanking new. She responded to his every touch, and she'd never let him down.

Swinging himself ashore, he untied the heavy mooring ropes, then returned to the cockpit and eased the gear lever into reverse. He could hear the propeller biting into the still water, and lines of salty foam streamed down either side of the hull. He maneuvered the sixty-foot boat in a gentle arc backwards.

The hull glided through the man-made rock entrance of the marina, and Ben put some distance between the boat and the breakwall before going forward and playing out the dinghy until it bobbed about fifteen yards astern.

"It's just you and me, girl," he told his boat, and settled himself behind the wheel. He nudged the yacht into its plotted course with his bare feet on the spokes and took the time to enjoy the predawn sea and sky.

Because what was life for if not taking the time to enjoy it? He'd learned that lesson the hard way, when his startup programming business took over his life. Running an empire left no time to enjoy anything. Human resources, corporate taxes, asset mainte-nance. There were people out there who thrived on managing those aspects of a large company, but Ben wasn't one of them.

A milky glow inched over the horizon to the east, and the dark shape of Ballena lay like a giant sleeping whale on the sea's surface. The headway of the *Silver Girl* turned the morning breeze into a balm of salt and cool on his face. He pointed his nose into it and drew in a lungful.

The past few weeks had been hectic. Ben had thought his years of fourteen-hour workdays were behind him when he sold out of RyanCorp. But dealing with his finance team, and playing endless rounds of golf with his dad...who knew being out of work would be so arduous? Then he'd spent a few days sourcing equipment for the environmental group he was supporting, buying electronics and cabling, reading up on submersible animal tags and infrared cameras. It had been all go. He grinned. Okay, he'd kind of enjoyed being busy. Being creative.

The first months after he'd sold out, he'd gone to ground in the boatyard, immersing himself in restoring the *Silver Girl* so he could keep to the terms of his sell contract. And, yeah, maybe he'd spent some time licking his wounds over his ex-girlfriend's rapid departure. Keeping out of the internet security business for twelve months hadn't seemed such a biggie when he'd signed it. But it had been tough. Tougher than he'd expected.

It was lucky for him he'd met Pablo and Maggie

on his first sail down into the Caribbean. Lending a hand in their turtle conservation project had been just the project he needed to fill his time once the *Silver Girl* was released from drydock and afloat once more, fully restored. And his twelve-month work restriction would be lifted in just two weeks' time. Not that he was counting the days ...

SABRINA GROANED. A kaleidoscope of jarring, clashing colors spun across the inside of her eyelids, and her head felt like it was about to explode. She felt dizzy and disoriented. The world was rocking. She groaned on a wave of pain and nausea and rolled her head to be comprehensively sick.

"Oh my god."

She lay back, spent. The awful feeling in her stomach had abated but the world was still rocking. She decided to risk opening her eyes, then rapidly closed them against the blinding glare of overhead sun. It felt like a needle dipped in burning pitch had pierced her optic nerve.

She waited for the rocking sensation to stop, trying to work out where on earth she was. She was hot, she knew that much. She was more than hot. Her mouth felt as though it was lined with sandpaper. Her skin was on fire. Bringing a trembling hand up to shield her eyes so she could open them in the glare took all her strength. Slowly, concentrating simply on breathing and lying still, she managed to open her eyes under the shadow of her hand. Taking her time to get used to the light, she gradually focused on the sky that appeared between her fingers. It was a blue so bright it was almost white. The brilliant orb of sunlight danced to and fro, high in the sky.

She must be dizzy. Or hallucinating. Why on earth would the sun dance about like that? Flopping her arm across her forehead, she gave up wondering where she was, and concentrated instead on what she could remember. She had been for a predawn stroll through the marina, that much was certain. She could remember enjoying the night air and the calm order of the yachts in their berths, but after that was a blank. Was she on the marina? It would explain the sunlight and why she was so hot. But wouldn't someone have walked past by now and woken her up?

She'd just have to sit up. Whimpering slightly as the pain in her head grew into a royally plus-sized hammering, she slowly rolled on to her front so she could lift herself up on her arms. Peering out between the bangs of hair that fell over her face, she looked down on to rough blue fabric. How strange. That looked like boat canvas. Just as the thought slid through her mind, a wave of salt spray threw itself over her back, its coolness startling against her blisteringly hot skin. With growing panic, she lifted her head and took in the blue canvas that stretched to reach a thick white rubber border. Beyond the border was a limitless view of the open ocean.

"Oh heavens," Sabrina whispered as the enormity of her situation struck her. "I'm all at sea!"

4

*B*en flicked a glance at his watch. Nearly eleven. The forward motion of the yacht under motor made reading the wind deceptive, but even so, he rather thought the afternoon trade wind had started to blow. It would be a relief to turn the motors off. There was nothing as peaceful as a yacht pulling gamely through the water under her filled canopy of sail.

He decided to check his emails before he cut the engine; the boat would soon move out of range of the broadband towers that fringed the larger islands of the Caribbean. Communication with the outside world would be patchy for the greater portion of his journey.

He frowned at the urgent one he found there. Crap. He hated emails from his lawyer. He particularly hated them when the subject line included the words, *Look out, pal. Lawsuit headed your way.*

What now? He scrolled down through the email, ignoring the attachments for the moment. The gist of it didn't take long to read. The new owners of Ryan-Corp were suing him for breaching his restraint of trade agreement. They had an investigator on his tail, who they'd be willing to call off in return for a quick settlement.

He fired off a quick response. *This is bullshit. Find out what you can, but you know, and I know, I've not breached it. Looks like it's time you started earning some of that handsome retainer I pay you. No settlement.*

He hit *send* and cursed when his laptop informed him he had no internet connection. Slamming the lid closed, he headed back up. Time to kill the engines and let the wind take over. Maybe some of his anger at the new directors of RyanCorp would be blown away by the breeze.

Some of his colleagues had scoffed at his decision to use traditional methods for rigging the sails on his luxury yacht. He had ignored them. Technology was his plaything; his college friends might even call it his mistress. But there was a time and a place for it, and besides, he was a man who enjoyed contrasts, who appreciated change. To Ben's mind, tradition was best for the love of his life, *Silver Girl.* He thought of the luxury gin palaces afloat whose skippers trimmed their sails by pushing buttons from their air-conditioned saloons and shook his head. When the *Silver Girl* needed a sail hoisted, it was going to be done the correct way, with the halyard wrapped around a mast winch and hauled up by muscle and brawn.

The sweat was beading at his temples and in the small of his back by the time he had raised the mainsail and jib, and Ben blew out a breath. This was thirsty work. And cathartic. He felt calmer about the email. Pissed off, yes, but calmer. His lawyer would be able to handle it. He promised himself a beer out of the cooler as soon as he was done with the sails, then turned his efforts to the mainsheet. When both sails were set, he lifted the bottom of the T-shirt he'd put on when the sun's rays started to burn and wiped his face. He stepped behind the wheel and kept an eye on the compass reading as his fingers closed over the motor controls. Turning off the motor would change the set of the yacht, and the autopilot would need a nudge. Easing back on the throttle, he listened as the diesel pulse of the motors faded into nothing before switching the ignition key into the *off* position.

Silence.

Ben closed his eyes briefly, a smile of content-ment playing across his face. Silence, but for the swish of water along the hull of *Silver Girl* and the creak and twang of the spare halyards against the mast. Silence, but for the—

"Help!"

His eyelids snapped open. "What the hell?"

The faint cry sounded again, and he spun on his heel to face the stern of the boat.

"Help!"

His eyes fastened on a small movement in the dinghy being towed behind the yacht. Squinting in the glare of the noon sun, he shook his head in disbelief. There was someone in it! As he watched, stunned for the moment into stillness, he saw the small figure lean weakly to one side and retch violently into the foaming water.

Stifling a curse, Ben grasped the spokes of *Silver Girl*'s wheel and turned the yacht into the breeze to spill the air out of the sails. He stabbed the new coordinates into the autopilot to keep the boat at a relative standstill. Pulling the dinghy in was going to be hard work even with the yacht hove to.

Giving a quick glance around the horizon to check there were no other boats in the near distance into which *Silver Girl* could collide, he turned his attention to the dinghy.

The small, rubber-sided boat was tossing about in the open seaway. It lay off the stern a distance of about fifteen yards. Blowing out a deep breath, he jumped down to the small timber swimming platform on the stern, braced his feet, and started hauling on the salt-swollen rope. His mind danced with the impossibility of finding a person in his dinghy fifty miles out to sea. A dozen ludicrous scenarios occurred to him and were summarily dismissed as he worked on the rope, hand over hand.

Only a few more feet. The rubber rim of the dinghy cannoned into the swimming platform with a dull scrape, and he lashed the rope into quick figure-eights over the bollard. His eyes fell on the figure lying prone on the bright-blue canvas cover that protected the dinghy's engine cover and controls from the salt spray. It was a girl, that much was certain. She lay curled in the fetal position, her hair a black tangle covering her face. The blue of her sodden dress blended perfectly with the dinghy canvas. By accident or design, he wondered cynically as he reached down to haul her out.

Dropping to his knees, he slid a hand under her shoulders and dragged the upper half of her body over the rubber edge and onto the swimming platform. She was a dead weight. Her head lolled weakly to one side, and he heard a low whimper come from her throat.

"Hang on, sweetheart. I've got you."

He grunted as he adjusted for her weight and eased her a little farther onto the swimming platform. He swayed lightly as the yacht pitched with a wave, sending a surge of cool water up through the swimming platform and over them both. He grabbed a handrail until the pitching movement ceased. The last thing he needed to do right now was fall off the boat. He eyed the stainless-steel ladder with misgiving. Carrying an unconscious body up there was not something he had taken into consideration when he had designed the refit of his boat.

Sighing, he grasped the girl firmly by the waist and slung her over his shoulder in a fireman's lift, then rose to his feet. Holding the steel ladder with one hand, he set a foot on the bottom rung.

"Here goes nothing," he muttered, and struggled, cursing, up to the deck, before clambering down the internal steps into the darkness of the saloon with his cargo. Dispatching the girl onto one of the upholstered bunks in the interior, he dashed back upstairs to get the yacht underway.

He didn't care who the hell she was, or how desperate she was to make his acquaintance, he was damned if he was going to let his sails flog in the stiffening breeze for any longer than was strictly necessary. With practiced ease, Ben released the dinghy into the yacht's wake once more, before taking the helm and allowing the Caribbean trade wind to coax the *Silver Girl* onto her graceful tack.

5

*S*abrina woke from a deep and troubled sleep to find herself lying in a bed, staring directly at a porthole.

"Why would a window be round?" she muttered. A dull ache above her temple sent her fingers flying to investigate, and she probed gently at the swollen bruise she found there. Memories came flooding back. She had whacked her head on something and been knocked unconscious. The next thing she knew, she had been bouncing about in the smallest vessel she had ever seen, in the middle of a very large ocean. She frowned, then instantly regretted it as her face shrieked in protest. She traced her fingers over her face, gingerly feeling the puffiness about her eyes and mouth. Her hands looked like lobster claws even in the dim light of the room she was in. She must be horribly, horribly sunburned.

Pushing back the sheet to check on the state of her legs, she became instantly aware of one perturbing fact. She was dressed in a very large and very unfamiliar T-shirt.

She swallowed and plucked nervously at the fine fabric with her fingertips. She could remember shouting for help when she had regained consciousness and seen the yacht towing the dinghy. She had a vague memory of being carried out of the scorching sunshine and into a dark, cool, comfortable place. She must be on the yacht, which would explain the round window, the lurching sensation. But everything else was a blank. Including, she thought darkly, exactly how she came to be wearing some strange shirt.

Holding her breath, she sneaked a quick peak inside the collar. Heavens above, it just got worse. Not a stitch of underwear to be seen.

She lay back on the pillows. You great blundering oaf, she thought. What mess have you got yourself into now? Heaving a sigh, she inched herself up the pillows. She was in a cabin of some sort, all varnished timber and navy cushions, with boxes and duffle bags piled high all over the floor and spare bunk. She noted with relief a large mug of water and paracetamol tablets had been left on the small bedside table

"I suppose that's a good sign," she croaked, her voice hoarse from dehydration. Supplying beverages and pain relief wouldn't be part of the modus operandi of kidnappers. She decided to be optimistic and assume she hadn't been rescued by a gang of debauchers of women. Coaxing two tablets into her mouth, she swallowed them down with a long drink of the blessedly chilled water.

"Oh. Heavenly," she said, lifting the beaded glass to her forehead and relishing the feel of cold glass on her heated skin. She sank back into the pillows, giving the tablets a chance to work their magic. If only her rescuers had had the forethought to provide her with a saline drip, she'd be able to make an even speedier recovery.

When she could feel the painkillers swimming their way through her various aches and pains, Sabrina steeled herself to get out of bed. It was time to make the acquaintance of her rescuers and find out the true extent of the hot water she had landed in.

BEN TOOK a few steps up the varnished stairs from the saloon to the cockpit so he could stick his head out of

the hatch and give the horizon a quick scan. All was well, he noted, and returned to the chart table, where he plotted the route he would follow over the next few days to arrive at Anguilla. As his fingers worked the split ruler and compass, his mind dwelled on the girl currently occupying his guest quarters. She had been in a sorry condition when he'd pulled her out of the dinghy. Exposure to the morning sun had reddened her skin dramatically, and she had been so dehydrated she could barely croak. He had forced water into her mouth and laid cold strips of fabric on the worst of her sunburn, but had deemed that the most he could do until she woke up.

His mouth twitched with amusement as he imagined how she would feel when she woke minus her dress and in one of his T-shirts. Peeling her out of the salty clothing had been an act of mercy, he thought to himself with a chuckle. "Divine mercy," he murmured under his breath, his fingers slipping momentarily from the compass as a raw vision of lusciously curved female flesh swam before his mind's eye.

Shaking his head to rid it of the image, he turned his attention back to the course he was supposed to be plotting. Since leaving Ballena at dawn, the *Silver Girl* had made a slow passage north in the light morning breeze and was only now clearing the small island of Barbados. It was another 120 miles northeast to Anguilla. With a bit of luck, the wind would swing soon, and he'd be able to drop the yacht's course down into a reach which would make for a fast and comfortable passage. If they managed a speed of six to eight knots they could be in Anguilla by the following afternoon.

Glancing at his watch, he saw it was time for his radio check in. Picking up the mike for the VHF radio, he began calling Pablo.

"Papa Alpha Bravo Lima Oscar, this is *Silver Girl*, do you copy? Over."

"*Silver Girl*, this is Papa Alpha Bravo. I'm reading you loud and clear. Ben, what's your position?"

He grinned as Pablo's booming voice roared out of the tiny speaker. He quickly gave his latitude and longitude, then asked the question that had been worrying him. "How're the nests?"

He heard a clatter of static over the airwaves before Pablo's voice came through. "Shit, man. Veronica's down there now. Two more nests destroyed last night."

He rubbed his forehead. The sooner he got back to Anguilla the better. "Hang in there. I've got the equipment on board."

"Roger that," said Pablo.

"You'd better change my chart sheet as well, pal,"

Ben said into the handset. "It's no longer a solo journey. *Silver Girl* has two P.O.B."

The answering radio chat followed a distinct pause. "Did you say you had two people on board?"

"Affirmative."

He let Pablo stew over that for a moment, before adding dryly, "It would seem that I have a stowaway."

"What?" The static of the radio couldn't disguise the surprise in Pablo's voice. "A stowaway? Do you want me to contact the authorities?"

Ben closed his eyes, dwelling for a second on the sleeping body in his guest cabin. He cleared his throat. "I can handle it, Pablo," he said into the handset. "*Silver Girl* out."

He slid the handset back onto its cradle and looked thoughtfully at his sun-browned hands. That was the problem. Handling his stowaway was about all he'd been able to think of since he'd unwrapped her from her sea-logged clothes. Hell. Handling her was where his thoughts had started. Where his thoughts had finished was a different matter entirely.

"Hello."

The husky voice stopped his thoughts dead in their tracks, and he spun around in his seat. Oh hell, he thought weakly. He was in serious trouble. This girl was gorgeous. Even with skin burned to the color of caramelized pumpkin, she looked so delectable he could feel the bones in his body melting. Her hair was the truest of blacks, and she had obviously made an attempt to smooth the ravages of the morning's tangles out of it. It framed her face before falling in a sheer drop out of sight behind her shoulders. And what shoulders. The T-shirt he had bestowed on her sat crookedly over her collarbones, exposing pale skin the color of a new moon. His eyes dipped to the generous curves which thrust his T-shirt out in a way that it had never been thrust out before, and he skidded his eyes upwards to her face. Inanimate, her body had had the power to enthrall, but standing here, conscious, breathing in that way...well, damn.

He shook his head clear and got a grip on his wandering thoughts. Fixing his gaze on the Atlantic blue of her eyes, he finally noticed the trepidation with which she was regarding him, and he forced himself to think. She was a stunner, all right, but she had maneuvered her way on board his boat in pretty questionable circumstances. He'd had more than a few crazies try and wangle their way on board. As big as the Caribbean was, it wasn't big enough to hide his identity, or the news of the big cut of profit he'd walked away with when he sold his company. Hitching a ride in his dinghy was pretty extreme, but who knew what lengths a mercenary woman would go to? His best course of action was to keep her at a distance until they docked in Anguilla, where she could be firmly placed ashore.

6

*S*abrina swallowed convulsively, barely aware of her various aches and pains as the man seated in front of the radio turned to face her. She couldn't believe it. Her breath lodged somewhere painfully in her breast. Her rescuer was the man she had bumped into on her way back to her hotel the previous night.

"You," she breathed.

"I beg your pardon?"

A tawny eyebrow lifted in query, and she frowned. Did he not recognize her? Granted, last night she hadn't looked like a boiled lobster. But still.

"I...um." She stammered to a close. What was happening here? Her brain didn't usually have this much trouble throwing a sentence together. Gripping a varnished handrail, she began again.

"I ran into you last night," she managed. "On the street outside my hotel."

The blond Adonis chewed on his lip for a moment before answering her, the expression in his eyes unreadable. "If you'd wanted to come aboard, you could've just asked," he said, his eyes dropping to linger on the length of T-shirt and even longer length of exposed leg beneath its hem. "Stowing away in the dinghy was a rather desperate way of getting my attention, wasn't it?"

Sabrina gasped. Getting his attention?

"Not to mention dangerous," he continued.

What? Was he serious? Could this man really be saying what she thought he was saying? Of all the crazy, lunatic ideas she had ever heard, this one took the crumpet. She almost laughed, but shivered instead as she saw the way his eyes lingered on her lightly clad body. Could have just asked, indeed. No doubt women concussed themselves and threw their unconscious bodies in his dinghy on a daily basis. She could feel the blood rushing to her head as anger and indignation warred for supremacy.

"Well, Captain," she said, in as icy a tone as she could manage. "Thank you for those kind words. It would seem it is not enough that I have just suffered from an horrific ordeal, nearly drowning, not to mention the dehydration and concussion and probably skin cancer, all because some fool decided to design this boat with a whacking great tree stump sticking out the front of it, for unsuspecting people to walk into. It does not appear to be enough that I have spent the morning being vilely ill and in mortal peril. No, it would seem that I have now to endure being rescued by some ignorant and chauvinistic philistine who thinks I have done all of this to myself on purpose just so I can hook a ride on this boat. For your information," she finished, crossing her arms with a sniff, "I'm not interested. Your virtue is safe."

She tried to reel herself in. Okay, it had been a bit of a blow to discover Captain Handsome was a jerk, but she didn't need to overreact about it. She had more pressing issues to deal with. Like getting back to Ballena. And antagonizing the captain might not be the best way to achieve that.

She choked back her outrage and schooled her features into the calm demeanor she used on drunks at the triage station on Saturday nights at St. Joseph's. "Why don't we start again? My name's Sabrina."

The captain nodded. "Sabrina. Like the witch."

"No. Not like the witch," she said repressively. "And you are?"

He leaned into the chart table as the boat canted over an ocean swell and smiled. "You can call me Ben."

Sabrina looked around, down towards the front of the boat where cabin doors remained shut. "And the rest of the crew? Where are they?"

He shrugged, shoulders rippling under the thin gray of his T-shirt. "Oh, there's no one else on board. Just you and me."

Her jaw dropped. She was alone? On a boat with just this man for company? A zillion miles out to sea with packs of marauding sharks swimming hungrily between her and the nearest scrap of land?

He smiled at her then, a long, slow smile that began in the corners of his eyes and ended somewhere deep in the pit of her stomach. She stared at the lazy curl of his mouth and couldn't blink. She felt winded and wasn't entirely sure if she still had a pulse. She shook her head, trying to break the hypnosis of attraction.

Breathe, you fool. The rational part of her knew that at some point her carbon dioxide levels were going to reach the point of either forcing her to drag some air into her lungs or making her black out. It was the irrational side of her that worried her. It couldn't care less whether she ever breathed again, just so long as she could keep the wattage of that smile burning straight in her direction.

She began to think she'd spoken too soon when she'd promised his virtue was safe.

❀

BEN REACHED into a chest cabinet and pulled out a couple of water bottles. "Thirsty?"

"Like a camel in the desert."

She slid the lid from the bottle he offered her and upended it, pulling at the cold water inside. He let his eyes linger on her face as she drank, then drifted them down over the cords of her neck, the over-large neckline of his shirt to the body below.

Fanciful images of sirens and mermaids flitted across his mind's eye, but he banished them with a snap. He wasn't averse to a little female company— particularly female company that was as delectable as his little stowaway witch—but usually he was the one doing the inviting. This woman's unorthodox arrival on his boat had him feeling unsettled. He was having a hard time believing she was here by accident.

The water finished, Sabrina set the empty bottle aside on the counter. She raised blue eyes to his. "You're still here."

"I beg your pardon?" Was she concussed? She didn't seem to be making any sense.

"I was hoping this had all been some horrible dream brought on by drinking unboiled water, but, alas, I see it isn't."

He felt his mouth twitch. Okay, so he was enjoying having a suspicious stowaway on board. Was that a crime? "I've never known anyone to get quite so sunburned during a dream before."

She grimaced. He could see the thoughts flitting over her expressive face.

"I guess since you are the only one on board, I have you to thank for pulling me out of the dinghy and providing the cold water and medicine. Thank you."

She cast a glance downwards, and he found himself charmed by the sudden flush that darkened her already pink face.

"Oh, er...and the T-shirt. Much appreciated. Very kind."

"Don't mention it."

He turned abruptly away from her and began to climb the ladder to the deck. The less he thought about stripping her out of her clothes, the better. Keep his distance, drop her ashore in Anguilla, he reminded himself. That was the plan.

"I've got a boat to sail, so I suggest you make yourself comfortable down here in the shade. If you fancy some food, help yourself. If you can wait, I'll be having lunch in an hour or so." He tapped his hand on the chest freezer inset into the counter. "There's plenty more water."

"Hang on a second."

He paused and looked back at her.

"Have we turned around? How long until we're back in Ballena?"

He blew out a breath. He doubted this was going to go well. "We're not headed back to Ballena."

She stepped closer to the stairs to stare up at him, a frown on her face. "What do you mean we're not headed back? I've got to get back. You can't kidnap me."

He smiled. Dangerously. "I think you mean rescue."

She gaped at him, eyes wide. "Ben. Please. I can't just disappear."

"Sweetheart, you should have thought of that before you stowed away on my dinghy. I'm on a schedule, and there's no turning back."

Ben turned his back to her and carried on up the stairs to the helm. She could stew on that for a while, he thought. She wasn't the only one with plans and responsibilities, and he had people counting on him. He stood in his cockpit and surveyed his yacht. The wind had kicked up a knot or two. The sails were full, and the deck slanted to leeward as the *Silver Girl* pushed through the ocean.

He left the autopilot on—even he could admit it steered the boat better than he could—and turned his attention to the crate of equipment he had stored under the cockpit table. The aft deck wasn't an ideal workshop, as the wind took everything that wasn't held down, and the table wasn't level when the boat was under sail, but he could work around it. He rolled out a non-slip mat to protect the varnish, then slid out his tools. Batteries. Wire. Drill. Screwdrivers. He opened a storage hatch and pulled out the fiberglass mold he'd had the boys in the chandlery knock up for him while he was in port and turned it upside down to continue tinkering with the camera housing.

He was pretty chuffed with his idea. When Pablo had told him of the troubles the turtle conservation project was having, he'd had a flash of memory from a nature documentary watched years ago. He'd make a security camera that looked like a rock. And getting his hands back into electronics, creating a device from scratch, with no blueprint, no how-to guide pushing him from A to B along the shortest possible route, was more fun than he'd anticipated. He'd experimented with lenses, battery power, mobility, wireless range, and had enjoyed every stage of his creation. And he felt pretty good knowing his work was for an environmentally proactive purpose.

The turtle nests on the island were being disturbed night after night. Pablo and his girlfriend Maggie rostered themselves and their volunteers on night duty when they could but there weren't enough of them to mount a twenty-four-hour surveillance. This was the reason he was in a hurry to get back to Anguilla. They were counting on him to help work out who or what was disturbing the turtle nests.

Birds, fire ants, lizards, wild pigs and dogs...the turtles had plenty of natural predators. But the rumors Pablo had been hearing about a gang of thieves who were raiding nests to sell eggs on the black market was what had him really spooked. The Caribbean islands were home to a lot of people, many of them living off what they could catch or grow. Selling turtle eggs on the black market, illegal poachers stood to make hundreds of dollars in cash from a single night's poaching. A fortune.

Ben tightened the last screws and set the fiber-glass camera housing back on the table. It wasn't perfect yet, but as a prototype, it would do. The camera parts were still boxed up in the quarter berth below decks. He'd wait until the boat was at anchor before he installed the lens in the waterproof casing: cameras and saltwater weren't a happy union.

He gave the controls a once-over and scanned the sea. All was clear, so he packed away his project, set the time on his watch for twenty minutes and settled in against the squabs for a snooze. Sailing the *Silver Girl* single-handed required the ability to snatch short chunks of sleep when he could. He closed his eyes and a vision of Sabrina standing at the foot of the saloon stairs, looking indignant, crossed his mind. He ran a hand over the stubble that was roughening his jaw. Either she was a damn fine actress, or she really had fallen by accident into his dinghy. His plan was prudent: keep his distance, drop her ashore in Anguilla. Maybe he'd have to throw the T-shirt of his that she was wearing into the nearest thrift store drop-off, and race back out to sea before his self-control started to waver.

Definitely the prudent thing to do, he mused. That was the problem. Playing it safe was not how Ben had developed one of the leading internet security firms in the northern hemisphere. He sighed. And there it was: the root of the problem. He was bored. He didn't cope overly well with endless hours of free time. The turtle conservation project kept him busy from time to time, but it had students, it had Pablo and Maggie leading it. It didn't need him.

Perhaps he had been rash selling his company. The twelve-month restraint of trade clause had given him too little to do. Way too little, if he was seriously contemplating playing games with a beautiful stranger who had stowed away on his boat. His thoughts flitted to his ex-girlfriend, who'd dumped him for a high-flying city boy the second he'd stepped down from being the boss of RyanCorp. Who knows how long she'd had an alternative boyfriend waiting in the wings. Women could be trouble. Particularly women who were hiding something. What was the cliché? Better safe than sorry.

He felt the wind ruffling through his hair and smiled. Would the world end if he said to hell with safe? Time would tell about the sorry.

7

Sabrina set the frosty can of soft drink on the teak deck beside Ben, giving it a good thunk as she did so in the hope it would wake him from his doze. She frowned down at him. Relaxed, his face had lost none if its appeal. Her fingers involuntarily stretched out to smooth a wayward tuft of hair that was blowing about his face. Just as her fingertips were about to meet the skin of his forehead, his lashes flew open and a razor-sharp blue gaze locked on to hers. She gasped as long, sun-bronzed fingers clamped about her wrist.

"What are you doing?" he murmured, his voice deep and husky with sleep.

She froze. Good question. What was she doing?

"I was waking you up," she said sharply, taking a rapid step backwards and moving as far away from his physical presence as she could within the confines of the yacht's cockpit. "I heard an alarm going off up here. Surely sleeping at the wheel isn't in your job description, Captain?"

He smiled lazily at her. "It is when the autopilot's driving, sweetheart."

She frowned at him. "Shouldn't you be keeping an eye out for submerged reefs and container ships and other hazards?"

Ben picked up his sunglasses from where they had slid down onto the cushioned bench beside him and slid them on.

"Thanks for the tip," he said, before lounging back down across the cushions on his side of the cockpit, crossing his arms behind his head and subjecting her to a thorough scrutiny.

Sabrina blushed. The gall of the man. It was almost as huge as his sex appeal. She closed her eyes briefly and ran a nervous tongue over her sunburned lips. He had to take her to shore and let her off this boat. She didn't care how big his damn yacht was, it wasn't big enough for her, him, and her suddenly volcanic libido.

Perhaps the sunburn had done it, burned off a layer of prudence at the same time it was burning off a layer of her skin. She couldn't remember feeling so flustered and breathless about a guy since her crush on the instructor at Pony Club when she was eight.

Boys, men...she knew them, worked with them, she'd dated a few. But her reaction to Ben was of a different order, like he possessed the one unique attribute her hormones had been waiting for.

She wondered again why Ben hadn't felt the need to turn the boat around when she was rescued. She'd spent the last hour in the cool dark of the saloon wondering. No one knew where she was. She had nothing but her bikini and her beach frock, both currently a wet mess on the floor of the bathroom in her cabin. No shoes, no phone, no identification. If Antonia's island-hopping plans fell through—and Antonia's man-plans often *did* fall through at the last minute, usually accompanied by some catastrophe—and she couldn't find Sabrina, she'd panic.

No, Sabrina would have to make him change his mind. She gestured to the can of drink forming a little ring of condensation on the ledge behind Ben's head.

"I brought a drink up for you," she said, to get the discussion started. "It must be thirsty work sitting out here in the sun all day."

He flicked a thoughtful glance in her direction as he reached over to the can, pulled its ring top open, and took a long drink. "Thanks," he said.

She pursed her lips. "Think of it as an olive branch."

"An olive branch? Well now, this is interesting,"

Ben said, setting the can down and looking at her expectantly. "Please, go on."

She frowned. "What do you mean, go on?"

He smiled at her. "I'm assuming you're only offering me an olive branch because you're expecting me to do something for you. So what is it?"

Sabrina glared at him. Why did he have to be so infuriating? Was it absolutely necessary for him to make her beg? Surely it was obvious she wanted to get back to dry land. She flashed gritted teeth in his direction and hoped her expression of fury could be mistaken for a polite smile.

"Ben, I'm sure it hasn't escaped your attention that I'm currently trapped on board this boat. I have no money, no clothes, and am getting farther and farther away from my hotel room as we speak. Will you please alter your arrangements so I can be dropped off at the nearest port?"

He took another swig of his drink and eyed her over the rim of the can. "You know, I'm almost inclined to believe you."

Sabrina bit back a pithy swear word that she hadn't realized was in her vocabulary. "Of course you can believe me," she said impatiently. "You're not still clinging to the ridiculous idea that I stowed myself away in that dinghy on purpose, are you?" Shaking her head, she sighed and got to her feet, swaying abruptly as a passing wave made her lose her balance momentarily.

"Look Ben," she entreated him. "I don't know you, and I don't know what axe you have to grind, but would you please do the right thing and get me back to land? I'm going back downstairs to lie down. All this sun up here is making me feel giddy. I'd appreciate it if you'd let me know your decision."

"Wait."

She turned back at the command. Ben's face was inscrutable, his eyes unreadable behind his sunglasses.

"I could take you back to Ballena, but it would mean a rough couple of days sailing into the wind. Or, we could continue to Anguilla, which we should reach tomorrow if this breeze hangs around, and you can fly back from there to Ballena." He looked around. "We're on a yacht. Sometimes the straightest line to where you want to go isn't the best direction to take. Sometimes the best direction to take is determined by the wind."

Sabrina pursed her lips. At last, some information. It would seem her olive branch was working. Whichever way she looked at it, there was going to be no quick rescue from her current predicament. She was going to be in close quarters with Ben for the next couple of days whether she liked it or not. It was a prickly situation.

She appreciated the fact that he had explained the choice between returning to Ballena or continuing to Anguilla. Maybe Captain Handsome wasn't the complete jerk she had made him out to be.

Would it hurt to find out, a rogue thought whispered?

She chewed her bottom lip. She had come to the Caribbean to take a break from the wreckage of her surgical career and the guilt that tormented her about her sister. Here she was, marooned on a boat in the middle of an ocean with a man who knew nothing of her background. All those months she had wished her problems would go away, but they hadn't. So she had gone away. Run away, if she was honest. And her problems had come with her.

Maybe being marooned at sea with a stranger for a few days, a man who had no idea who she was or what she was running from...maybe this was a chance to remember what it felt like to live without crushing guilt, without the sense of failure that had overwhelmed her. For a few days she could pretend to be an ordinary woman. Not a woman who had failed to save her sister. Not a woman who had lost the courage to continue with her career. Just a woman. At sea. On an adventure.

And then there was the other thing. Her physical reaction to Ben. Not once before had she experienced this primal surge of desire. Her senses were drowning in it. How would she control her reactions to him over the next two days?

A prickle of emotion started to uncurl in the corner of her subconscious, and it took Sabrina a moment to realize what the unfamiliar sensation was. Excitement.

Would the world end if Sabrina Gray deviated from the path she'd laid out ahead of her and had a bit of an adventure? Abandoned her normal caution for the first time in her life? She took a deep breath before committing herself to the journey ahead, feeling her heart thrum with an unfamiliar blend of anticipation and trepidation. She'd go where the wind took her.

"Anguilla it is."

---

8

*S*abrina passed an uncomfortable night in her bunk, waking abruptly in the gray dawn at a sudden noise. She lay still for a moment, gathering her thoughts. She was used to waking suddenly, usually in the grip of a nightmare. But no haunting images of death and disaster had visited her during the night. She'd slept uncomfortably, but she'd slept, and she was glad of it.

The boat was no longer traveling smoothly through the water, and the engine was on, its drumming sound coming up through the cabin floor. Her cabin was pitching and yawing, and she jumped as a carton slid from the pile on the twin bunk opposite her and landed with a thunk on the floor.

Well. Now she knew what had woken her up. She surveyed the scattering of boxes that had slipped from the other bed, then pushed back the sheet and climbed to her feet. She needed to brace herself against the bunk as the boat rose and fell.

Was she going to be seasick? Hopefully not...the unease in her stomach felt like hunger, not queasiness. Thank heavens. The thought of Captain Handsome having to hold back her hair while she disgraced herself over a bucket was too lowering to contemplate. She didn't want to feel indebted to her rescuer. True, he didn't seem like a kidnapper, not that she knew what kidnappers would seem like. True, he'd been kind, provided painkillers, food, shelter. But what else did she know about him other than the fact he stirred up her senses into a stew of lust?

Picking the boxes up, she read a label or two as she replaced them on the bunk. Ethernet cables. Lenses. Wire, clips, switches, solenoids. Hmm. Perhaps her host had interests other than cruising about the Caribbean looking like a modern-day Norse god.

She slipped into the cabin's tiny bathroom and looked in the mirror to inspect her sunburn. Well. She'd looked better, that was for sure. But there was definitely improvement from yesterday. The swelling in her face had gone down, and the redness had faded to a dull glow. Her forehead showed some signs of blistering; no doubt she'd be losing some skin there in the next few days. She eased the T-shirt down off her shoulder to inspect her neckline. The abrupt change from deep red to white still looked angry, but she could touch the burn now without it hurting.

Flipping the shower control to somewhere slightly north of tepid, she dragged off the shirt and used it to tie a makeshift turban over her hair. Brushing it out yesterday had been agony; she wasn't in a hurry to repeat the process today. The shower was sublime, even with the boat rolling so wildly that she had to wedge herself against the fiberglass wall. She turned her face into the water and let it run over her skin. She was starting to feel less like a rotisserie chicken and more like herself.

Mindful that water storage on board probably wasn't endless, she flicked the tap off and wrapped herself in a towel. She ran an eye over the drawers and hanging space in the cabin and decided to give them a thorough search. She was damned if she was putting that man's T-shirt back on.

The bathroom was well stocked with toiletries, and she helped herself, smoothing a liberal dollop of moisturizer over her burns. A storage drawer turned up a sarong and, miracle of miracles, her bikini which she'd tied to the inner handle of the brass porthole yesterday was dry. Her blue beach dress was dry too, but stiff with salt. She'd have to remember to wash it out in the shower later so she had something else to wear.

She took a last look at herself before she left the cabin. The sarong was a riot of color, an impractical confection of peacock blues and hibiscus orange, but it was a roomy piece of fabric, and she'd managed to wrap it around herself and secure it behind her neck. The end result was surprisingly neat. She combed the ends of her hair out and pushed it into a loose braid, with the help of a little loop of thin elastic that had been in one of the bathroom drawers, and nodded to herself in the mirror. She'd do.

The saloon was empty, so she made her way up the stairwell. Ben was at the helm, feet braced, hands spanning the huge silver wheel. The ladder steps up to the cockpit gave her ample time to drift her eyes over his bare feet and up tanned legs to the faded denim cutoffs he wore low on his hips. His chest was bare. She felt her pulse pick up a beat. His hair was wild, and his eyes as they met hers looked distant, as though his thoughts had moved beyond the two of them, beyond the boat.

She stepped over the hatchway and into the cockpit, hanging onto a winch to keep her balance. The world above was windy and gray, and the sea was churned into white-tipped waves. She almost felt a little cool, but then decided she was being ridiculous.

She was a Londoner, for heaven's sake. A gray sky in the Caribbean summer could not be considered cold.

"You okay? You're not seasick? I've got tablets downstairs somewhere if you are." Ben's voice lifted above the noise of the wind singing in the rigging and the low pulse of the engines.

She smiled, filling her lungs with the wet, salted air. She really was okay. "I'm great."

He smiled. "Okay then."

She walked along the length of the cockpit until she reached the seat behind the helm. Its canvas squabs were a little damp from sea spray, but she ignored the wetness and took a seat. Keeping her balance was too difficult standing. "What happened to the sails?"

Ben looked at her over his shoulder. "The wind's changed direction. It's coming straight at us from the direction we want to go in, so I pulled the sails in about midnight. We've been motoring since then, but it's getting a bit rough."

Sabrina nodded. "Those boxes in my cabin are flying all over the place."

"I'll fix it up later. I'm heading in to shore to get out of this headwind."

He pointed ahead, and she stood to look past him. A low island was not too distant. More of an atoll really, just a speck of land with a small thatch of green.

"I've anchored here before, so my GPS has the route in to the cove mapped." Ben tapped a finger on the instruments he had mounted on the helm. "We just need to follow the dots."

She leaned in to inspect the screen. A blue boat shape showed their position against the grid of sea and land. "Is it inhabited?"

HOLY DOOLEY, she smelled amazing. Ben slid his gaze down her shoulder and the smooth slope of arm as Sabrina leaned in next to him to inspect the screen of his GPS. Her hair was a dark rope of complicated plaiting, and it fell forward as she moved. He watched it swing and felt his lungs tighten. He'd had a long shift through the night, keeping watch on the weather and the autopilot. He was tired, but happily so. And his hunger had been steadily building since dawn. But that waft of Sabrina as she moved into him at the helm had all thoughts of sleep and food splintering.

Sex. That was what he wanted. A long slow morning of it. His eyes wandered over the sarong she had wrapped around herself. She looked exotic, like an English rose going to a fancy-dress party as a Polynesian princess. Long. Slim. With curves that made him think of the pleasures of unwrapping her sarong one tiny, revelatory inch at a time.

He snapped out of his lust-fueled daydream when he realized she'd had to repeat her question.

"Is it inhabited?"

"No, it's tiny. There's no fresh water either, so it's just a yachtie stop."

The approach to the atoll was through a gap in its fringing reef. Surly-looking waves were breaking over the coral to either side of the boat as the *Silver Girl* slipped through into the calm water within. The boat's motion grew easier immediately. As they motored in closer to the small outcrop of land, the wind that was sending rippling gusts across the surface of the lagoon eased. The yacht shuddered as Ben threw the motor into reverse to bring the hull to a stop. Seconds slid away, and then the anchor chain started rattling.

"Can you watch the anchor chain for me?" he asked.

"Sure. Up the front?"

He grinned. Sabrina was no yachtswoman. He could certainly eliminate itinerant yacht-hopper looking for a free ride from his list of possibilities about her past, if she didn't know where anchors were to be found on a boat. "Yes, up the front. I'll release the chain from here, you let me know when you see the red-painted links."

He hit the switch for the windlass as he watched her walk up to the front of the boat. The wind whipped at her sarong, and he caught a glimpse of thigh as the thin fabric snagged the breeze. Mind on the job, Ben, he told himself. "Any color yet?"

The links kept unfurling over the bow.

"Blue," called Sabrina, and a few seconds later, "okay, green."

Red was next. She lifted a hand. "Red's up."

Ben killed the windlass and the anchor noise came to an abrupt halt. He let the yacht settle and checked out the shoreline to get his bearings. A curl of beach hugged the inside of the atoll, and above it rose the small hill that was keeping them out of the wind. Its sides were covered in long grass, and the only trees were a cluster of palms at the far end of the beach.

The anchor was holding. He walked up the deck to the front of the boat and checked that the anchor chain was snug in its roller. Sabrina watched him, hugging her shoulders as a splatter of raindrops fell from the sky. A dense cloud was hanging low on the horizon, its belly dark with the promise of a deluge. Despite being midmorning, the day had grown gray and dim.

"Are we safe here?"

Ben cocked an eyebrow at her. "Sweetheart, we'd be safe out there. It's a rainstorm, nothing worse. I'm just checking the anchor's holding. This lagoon's a pretty tight fit for a yacht this size. We don't have a lot of swing room."

She frowned down at the anchor. "How can you tell it'll hold?"

"Relax. It's fine. The anchor's heavy, and so is the extra chain I laid down."

A roll of thunder undercut his words, and they both looked up at the sky as a flash of sheet lightning blazed in the cloud.

"How do you feel about pancakes?" he said, walking back to the helm and switching off the engine.

She smiled. "I could make a lifelong commitment to pancakes. Who's cooking?"

"I'll cook. You clean."

Taking a last look at the raincloud sitting snugly over their atoll, Ben followed Sabrina down the hatch into the saloon. Maybe over a meal he could get the answers to some of his questions. Like who she was. And what she was doing here on his yacht.

9

*R*ain hammered at the long windows of the saloon, but inside was snug and dry. Sabrina was surprised at how far the temperature had fallen. Ben had disappeared into a hatch to attend to something technical, so she took her time inspecting the saloon.

A kitchen nook curled to one side of the stairs, its cupboard fronts and appliances gleamingly new. A workstation sat opposite, with the digital displays of instruments blinking and computer screens glowing blue. The front of the saloon was taken up with lounge chairs in denim-colored velvet. Strip windows circled the saloon at eye height, but the view to the outside world was a whiteout of mist and rain.

She turned her attention to the computer open

on the workstation desk and wondered if there was an internet connection she could use. If she could email her hotel, they could let Antonia know she hadn't disappeared into thin air. Although, if Antonia had carried through with her plans to go island hopping with her dashing pilot, it wasn't likely her absence would be noticed for a few days.

She ran a finger over the mouse plate of the laptop, and the screen sprang into life. A code box asked for a password. Here goes nothing, she thought. She typed in the letters of the yacht's name: *silvergirl*, and hit enter. A disembodied female voice spoke out of the computer and echoed through a series of speakers dotted about the saloon.

"Ben, darling, someone is trying to break into your computer."

"Oops," said Sabrina.

She heard a sound behind her and jumped, her eyes locking on Ben's. "What the hell was that?"

He said nothing, just walked over to the workstation and slid the lid of his laptop shut. He was dangerously close and even more dangerously shirtless. He gave her a long look. "If you want to use my computer, you need to ask. Honey gets fractious when I let other people play with her."

"Honey?"

She was flustered. She felt embarrassed at having

been caught out trying to access his computer, and being caught by some fake female security system with the voice of a 1930s film star just made it worse somehow. But it was Ben's proximity that was really making her flustered.

"Sorry. I was thinking if we had internet I could email my hotel."

His hand stayed on the top of his laptop. Possessively. He shot her a look. "What are you really doing here, Sabrina?"

She looked up at him. She was standing so close she could see the way the blue of his eyes shot to green close up to the iris. His lashes were dark, and the creases in the corners of his eyes were paler than the skin surrounding them. They spoke of lazy hours outdoors in the sun. The expression in his eyes wasn't lazy, however. He looked serious. And wary. She lifted her hands, trying to suppress her frustration.

"You know why I'm here. I had an accident."

He nodded. "Yeah. So you've said. That's not what I'd describe as an adequate explanation."

"Nonetheless, it's the explanation I've given you. And I said it because it's true. What other possible reason would I have for endangering my life in your dinghy?"

"You weren't to know my winch was broken. The

marina office knew I was planning to leave that morning. Anyone watching would have seen me provisioning the boat. It wouldn't take a rocket scientist to figure out I was about to head out to sea."

She huffed. "Well I must be a long way from being a rocket scientist. I didn't know anything about your travel plans. I didn't inveigle my way aboard." She could feel herself getting angrier. Why on earth was her story so hard to believe?

"So if you're not a rocket scientist, what are you? Who are you?" Ben crossed his arms over his chest and leaned back, looking as though he had all the time in the world to hear a long and thorough answer.

What was she? Who was she? Sabrina paused and rubbed her face. What he didn't know was that these were the very questions she had been asking herself for weeks. Months. If she knew the answer, she'd tell him. If she could bring herself to acknowledge what she had become—a surgeon who couldn't practice, a doctor who couldn't look at blood—she would. She turned her head. She couldn't meet his gaze.

"I'm a woman on holiday. Trapped on a boat, trying to get the hell off. I'm sorry, but that's all I'm prepared to tell you."

He nodded. "Okay. Keep your secrets. For now. But I'll tell you one of mine. You ready?"

Baffled, she shot a glance up to his face. He stared down at her.

"I don't like having someone on board my boat that I can't trust. Someone is investigating me. My movements. Who I communicate with. Who I work for. And if I find out that that someone is you..." He paused and rubbed a hand over his jaw. "You're going to regret the day you decided to become a stowaway on the *Silver Girl*."

She dropped her gaze to the laptop that had started this conversation. How could she let him know that she wasn't doing any of those things without revealing the most secret of her vulnerabilities? She couldn't. That he didn't trust her hurt. She was surprised by how much. It just showed how far from okay she was that she no longer acted in a trustworthy way.

But she was holding back on details of her life because she didn't have the strength to acknowledge them, because she was weak. Ben didn't look weak at all. What sort of trouble could he be in, that would have him so suspicious? She cast a wary look at him. She had been thinking of him in terms of a pirate. Not because she thought he was one, but because the idea of it was romantic. Rum, pieces of eight, a balmy Caribbean breeze, and her own handsome pirate keeping her captive on a boat.

Her pulse raised a notch. She felt alarmed just

thinking about it. Surely he wasn't a drug runner? A wanted criminal? No. How many drug lords spent their time dispensing paracetamol and glasses of iced water to sunburn victims? If Ben was in trouble, it wasn't because he was a criminal.

"I'm not an investigator," she started to say, but her words drifted to a close and her breath hitched as she saw he didn't seem to be paying much attention to what she was saying.

His eyes had grown dark, and he took a step closer.

"You want to know another secret?"

She shifted on her bare feet and her hips bumped the chart table behind her. She wasn't trapped. She could push her way past him if she needed to, but...did she need to? The reckless voice in her head didn't think so; it was saying *Sabrina! This is so thrilling ... what's he going to do next?*

"There's no internet out here. No phone service either. It's just you and me. Whoever you are," he muttered, and his hand reached up and drew a finger along her collarbone and up the side of her neck.

She shivered. "What? Are we in some sort of Bermuda Triangle?" All thoughts of accusation and outrage had fled in that moment when his finger touched her skin.

He grinned, a flash of teeth and dimple in a sun-browned face. "I think we must be," he murmured, before he placed his other hand in the small of her back and pulled her sarong-clad body abruptly against his. "Because despite my doubts, I'm about to kiss you."

His voice was low, the murmur of a purring jungle cat, and he reached a hand up to pull on the thick tail of her plait. The tug of hair sent pinpricks of awareness over her, as did the brush of stubble against her cheek.

"Do you want me to stop?"

He leaned in closer, settling just enough of his weight against her that the rough denim of his shorts dug into her hip bones. She shut her eyes on a moan as his other hand slid slowly up her body, over the silk of the sarong covering the small of her back, to where bare skin met his fingers.

"Don't stop," she breathed, and realized as she said the words that reckless Sabrina was in charge. She wanted to fist her hands in his hair and pull him to her, to bury her face in his neck and taste.

His hands were warm on the skin of her back, their work-roughened callouses grazing against ribs, shoulder blades; she shuddered, and then his lips were on hers, and all her thoughts of *sure* or *not sure* shattered. There was no room in her head for anything but feeling. The rasp of stubble, their heated breath, the kick of heartbeat: his and hers. Sabrina cupped his neck to drag him closer and breathed little sounds of encouragement as his mouth feasted on hers. The blood in her veins felt like it was about to explode. She was on fire with need.

A strong arm looped over her shoulders and pulled her in closer to the heat. Her breasts pressed against his chest, her hips pushed against his. She ran a hand up his bare side, feeling the swell of muscle over ribs, the taut flesh of strong, healthy male.

The high-pitched noise she could hear behind her could have been signaling the end of the world but right there, right then, having the dickens kissed out of her by this blond pirate, she didn't care if her world did end.

Wait. She opened her eyes. There really was an alarm sounding just behind her head, from one of the army of machines plugged in above the chart table.

"Ben," she said sharply.

He lifted his head and looked at her, his eyes soft and sort of dreamy, and her heart did a little flippety-flop in her chest.

"The alarm."

His expression snapped into one of alertness. "Shit."

He reached around her to the chart table to tap a button. "Depth warning. Anchor needs checking." Then he charged up the stairs to the cockpit.

Sabrina watched him go. "Wow," she murmured to herself. And smiled. Wow indeed.

10

*F*at was sizzling in a pan and a warm cloud of vanilla and lemon had formed in the saloon by the time Ben had shortened the anchor chain and assured himself the *Silver Girl* was safe if the wind swung round again. He toweled the rain out of his hair on his way below deck, then leaned a hip against the island bench of the kitchen and watched Sabrina work. She had plates set on the table and a tower of crepes was steadily building on a serving platter near the stove. He watched her pour a thin stream of batter into the pan and swirl it around until the batter formed a thin round. She left it to sizzle and turned to the halves of lemon lined up on the cooking board. She shot him a look, and a thin band of color stained her cheeks.

"Do you have a juicer? I can't find one."

Okay. So they weren't going to talk about what had happened in the kitchen. The stand-off or the kiss. He could run with that for the moment. He reached over her head and opened a cupboard door.

"Why would I need a juicer when I've got a gallon of maple syrup?"

Sabrina frowned and pointed to the food she'd set out on the counter. "Pancakes. Lemon. Sugar. It's the holy trinity of breakfasts. Who messes with perfection?"

She turned back to the pan where the crepe was starting to bubble and gave it a flip with an expert flick of the wrist. Ben's eyebrows rose. Cooking skills. His stowaway was starting to look better and better. He found a jug, then squeezed the lemons she'd halved into it, tossing the skins and pulp into the sink. He pulled up the chest lid of the fridge and took out the butter, dug the maple syrup out of the pantry, and set them all on the saloon table. The soft hiss of the gas burner clicked off, and she brought over the plate of steaming crepes.

"One at a time or do you like them in a stack?" she asked, holding a fork poised over the plate.

He considered the hunger pangs gnawing at his stomach for about a millisecond. "Better make it a stack."

He smothered his pile with maple syrup and wolfed into it. Sabrina made a fuss of sprinkling her crepe with lemon and sugar, then rolling it into a sausage and sprinkling it with more lemon and sugar. He shook his head. "You've got a lot to learn about American pancakes."

She looked up. "What do you mean? You don't like my pancakes?"

"I love them. It's just we'd call these crepes. And maybe have them for dessert. An American pancake is served thick, like the heel of your shoe, with maybe some bacon and grits on the side."

She made a face. "I don't even know what a grit is. It sounds like someone forgot to wash the dirt out of a celery stalk."

"You've never had an all-American breakfast if you haven't had grits."

She helped herself to another crepe. "I'll take your word for it."

A squawk from the chart table had them both turning their heads. "*Silver Girl*, this is Papa Alpha Bravo. Do you copy?"

Sabrina's eyes opened wide as she looked across at him. "We can contact someone? I thought you said no phones, no internet?"

He got to his feet. "Radio. There must be a repeater station within range. It can vary a bit depending on the weather." He lifted the black speaker unit from its slot on the chart table.

"Pablo, this is *Silver Girl*, over."

"We've got trouble, Ben."

"What's up?"

"Two more nests destroyed last night. But we've seen tracks and..." the rest of the message dissolved into crackle and gibberish.

He waited for the noise to end then spoke into the transmitter. "Say again? You're breaking up."

A stream of static burst out of the speaker then silence.

"Pablo Alpha Bravo, this is *Silver Girl*. Do you copy?"

The silence resumed.

"Crap," said Ben. He turned to Sabrina and shrugged. "We might get some better reception once these rain squalls have passed."

She leaned back in the seat and eyed him. "Who's Pablo? And what trouble is he talking about? Is this related to your mystery investigator?"

Ben busied himself pulling mugs out of a cupboard while he considered what to tell her. "You want a coffee?"

She nodded, and he clicked the gas on under the kettle.

"Pablo's an ecologist. He runs a turtle conservation project at an isolated coral cay off the northernmost tip of Anguilla. He and his partner live there most of the year, and during the nesting and hatching seasons, they house volunteers to help them guard the nests and make sure the hatchlings get into the water."

"Sea turtles?"

"Yeah. The Caribbean is a nesting site for a lot of turtle species. Hawksbills, greens, leatherbacks. Turtles only nest where they were born, so as their nesting sites are destroyed, it impacts their numbers. They're all endangered, and the hawksbill is on the critical list. Ecologists have estimated its population has declined by eighty percent in recent years."

"And you're working for him?"

Ben grinned. "Sort of." He thought about his project stowed up on the aft deck. Could something as fun as hiding cameras in fake rocks be called working? "Pablo's a friend of mine. You know those boxes in your cabin? I'm helping him rig up some monitoring equipment. They don't have enough volunteers to keep an eye on the nests twenty-four-seven, so that's where I come in."

He poured hot water into mugs. "You take milk? It's out of a box, not the real stuff."

Sabrina made a little gagging noise. "Yes, I noticed that when I made the crepes. I'll take it black, thanks."

He handed her a mug, then sat back into the saloon seating, raising his legs so his feet were propped beside her on the opposite couch. Perhaps it was time he and Sabrina got to know each other.

Particularly since he knew it was only a matter of time before he kissed her again, despite his suspicions about what she was doing on board his boat. He had been inclined to believe her crazy story about falling into his dinghy until she'd had a go at getting into his laptop.

But now he was remembering his lawyer's words of warning in that last email: not to underestimate the lengths his buyers would go to if they thought they could squeeze some serious bucks out of him. He'd thought nothing of it at the time, as he had nothing to hide. But now?

Now he remembered how reluctant his stowaway had been to reveal anything about herself. And his brain was functioning again—the fat and sugar in his stomach had dulled his lustful urges—leaving him to wonder why she hadn't pushed at him more to head in to land. To sail closer to the coast so they could pick up a signal. Sure, he'd have been resistant. He really did have to be at the turtle project urgently. But that didn't explain why she'd let the idea go so quickly.

What reason would a woman have for being so easily persuaded to leave her life, her belongings, and sail north through the Caribbean on the word of a stranger?

He grinned, remembering the look on her face when Honey had thwarted her attempts to use his computer. Sure, she would need to email her hotel. But who else did she need to email? And about what? It was almost a shame they had no internet connection. He'd have been able to trace any email she sent regardless of how clever she was on a keyboard. Snooping about on the internet was his special skill, after all.

He needed to know a hell of a lot more about the siren who had landed on his boat. He eased his way into it by crossing his feet, allowing them to rest against the warmth of her thigh. He dropped his voice a notch. "Anything else you want to know?"

She blushed. She actually blushed. Perhaps it was the pallor of her natural skin tone, the contrast to the sleek darkness of her hair, but a flush rose to mottle her neck and stain her cheeks. Hmm. Clearly, he wasn't the only one who'd had the fuses in their brain blown by their earlier kiss.

He watched her struggle to regain her composure, open her mouth to ask another question, then close it again. Asking questions was a two-way street: maybe she thought if she asked about him, then he would ask about her. Which was totally his strategy. He rested his gaze on her, blue eyes in the porcelain-doll face, thick hair lying in a complicated plait down her shoulder. She looked wholesome. Honest. Just the sort of face that an investigative attorney would need to beguile their quarry into spilling the beans.

All right, he thought. Keep your secrets for the moment. He was in no hurry to find out. In fact, after this morning's little tryst in the kitchen, he was rather looking forward to peeling back the secret layers. Investigator or not, Sabrina had stirred him up, and anticipation was a buzz he could enjoy. For a while, anyway.

11

The rain had cleared, but heavy clouds choked the sky, and the light of late afternoon wasn't enough to lend color to the atoll in the lagoon. Sabrina would have liked to have stepped ashore, but Ben was in a hurry to get moving. Pablo's message from the turtle sanctuary clearly worried him.

"We've got to get the dinghy up on the davits. It's too rough to tow it, but the electric winch is playing up. Can you give me a hand?"

She snapped out of the reverie she'd fallen into while she surveyed their surroundings and stepped out from under the canvas awning onto the aft deck.

"Sure. What should I do?"

"We can winch it up onto its davits using the sailing winches, but they're manual winches. I need you to do one while I do the other, and we need to keep an eye on the ropes and make sure the boat's coming up evenly."

Ben jumped down onto the swimming platform and pulled the dinghy in close to the stern. "Hand me those ropes, will you?"

Sabrina passed down the ropes he was pointing to, and he shackled them into a pulley system that was rigged over the top of the dinghy.

"Now just pull on them to take the slack out."

He climbed back up to the deck and wound the ropes around two of the big silver winches bolted onto the stern. He passed her a massive handle. "The winch is self-tailing."

She looked at him blankly. "You are speaking a foreign language."

Ben scratched his head. "Okay. You wrap the rope around the winch three times, then push it into this guide." He matched his words with actions, then took the handle off her and slid it into the hole on the top of the winch. "The winch has two gears. So that means we wind it clockwise when it's easy to wind, but as the boat clears the water it's going to get heavy, so then we wind the other way."

"Okay. I can do that," Sabrina said, and moved in next to him, her hip bumping his in the narrow space at the winch. She ignored the little rush that came with the proximity.

Ben walked over to the other winch and did the same with his own rope. "Ready? Now we winch."

She wound in unison with him, surprised at how easily the dinghy started to lift. She kept her eyes on Ben as she wound, mirroring his movements. Did the man own any shirts, she wondered, watching his biceps flex and extend as he worked the handle. His skin was tanned to an all-over golden. She wondered what it would be like to be so free of responsibility that you could live out your life on the ocean, going where your whim took you.

The weight in her arms started to pull, and she noticed the nose of the dinghy was lower than the stern. "It's not even," she said.

"Switch to anti-clockwise," he said.

She was aware of him watching her, and she puffed with the effort it took to keep winding.

He seemed to be enjoying the spectacle. "Put your back into it."

She blew out a breath and kept going. This was worse than boot camp. At last the nose of the dinghy was high enough, and he joined in on his winch. The dinghy's rubber rim squeaked up against the stainless-steel arms of the davits.

"Good job."

Ben pushed down the jammer on his rope to keep it from slipping, then tied it off before coming over to do the same to hers. He glanced at his watch. "Okay, let's get this anchor up, and we're away."

"How long will it take us to reach Anguilla?"

"Maybe just before dawn? The wind's up, but it's from a good angle. We should get a pretty good ride heading northwest."

"Through the night?"

He ran a hand down her arm. "Hey. We'll be fine. The only tricky bit is getting out of this atoll, that's why it's best we leave now. It's low tide, which means the breakers let us know where the reef is. We'll motor out, then haul the sails up while we still have daylight to see. Then if the wind keeps doing what she's doing now, we'll have an easy sail through the night."

He leaned back his head and perused the sky. "I think it's going to clear. Maybe we'll see some stars."

She decided she'd take his word for it. The clouds still looked moody to her, sullen with unfallen rain, but perhaps storms did clear quickly in the Caribbean. And Ben was right about clearing the atoll: it had been easy. She stood on the prow and kept a hand pointed at the deep channel between the submerged reefs. Even setting the sails was done without a glitch, despite the way the boat began to pitch as soon as it cleared the calm of the lagoon. She helped him at the mast with the halyards, which she now knew were the heavy wires which hauled the sails up the mast. It wasn't until Ben went forward to adjust the foot of the jib that his evening plan for a balmy night sail under the stars went haywire.

She was at the helm, having nervously taken the wheel when he called her over.

"Keep your eye on the panel," he'd said, pointing at the digital numbers flicking on the small screen. The afternoon had faded into evening, and the glow from the screen had grown brighter as the dark descended. "We want to be headed north-north-west, which is 325 on the gauge. If the numbers go higher, steer to port a touch. Left. The numbers go lower, then take us a smidge starboard."

He went forward to mess about with sails and ropes, and the next thing she knew there was a muffled thud from the forward deck, followed by a loud curse, then silence.

"Ben?"

He didn't respond.

"Crap," Sabrina whispered, peering into the darkness ahead of the mast. The huge sail pulling the boat through the water gleamed palely in the dark, but nothing else moved. She put some lung-power into it.

"Ben!"

12

She was alone. At the wheel. On the deck of a sixty-foot yacht headed hell knew where.

What the blazes was she to do now? Her palms felt sweaty. Her stomach lurched. She flicked a look at the electronic screen. Keep it to 325 degrees. That was the instruction, so assuming she could steer it in a straight line, she wasn't going to be crashing into anything anytime soon. She hoped. The numbers had flicked low, into the 290s, so she experimented with a spin on the wheel.

The digits plummeted to 170. Crap. She badly wanted to panic about the reef she could be about to plummet the yacht into. The one that would rip the keel off and leave her, and her problems, afloat, alone, on the ocean. For the second time in a week.

She closed her eyes and thought about saying a tiny little prayer.

Wait a minute. The *Silver Girl* was a luxurious yacht. Perhaps it had power steering, like a car? She tried giving the huge wheel the tiniest of nudges, and sighed her relief as the numbers settled back at 325.

She could steer. Okay. Her next problem was going to be working out how to keep steering the boat in the right direction, but at the same time go forward and discover what had happened to Ben. The waves were tossing the boat about like it was a cork. As soon as she took her hands from the wheel, the direction would change; they could end up anywhere. Ben had talked of an autopilot, but she had no idea what it looked like or how to switch it on.

Perhaps she could tie the wheel in place? Lights spilling out of the hatchway to the saloon kept the cockpit well illuminated. She lifted the squab cushions to either side of the wheel and found storage compartments. With her hip bracing the wheel, she pulled on a ring handle and inspected the contents beneath. Tools. Sunscreen. A paperback novel with a ratty, salt-stained cover, and loads of rope. Letting out a breath, she hauled out a length and rigged up a rope securing the wheel to the saloon table. She watched the numbers on the display for a few seconds, saw them lower a little, then rise a little, relieved when they steadied in the mid 320s. Okay; not perfect, but their course was stable enough for her to run forward and take a quick look, then come back and check.

It wasn't until she had left the relative calm of the cockpit that she felt the full strength of the wind and waves. The yacht was hurtling through the water, canted to one side, its bow plunging through the swell. She made her way down the high side, keeping a firm grip on the rail. She wasn't imagining the temperature now: it was cold. Her sarong provided little protection against the sharp ocean breeze or the sprays of ocean that were being flung up over the deck.

"Ben?"

The wind whipped at her voice, sending it trailing back over her shoulder.

There was less to hold onto as she reached the front of the boat, but thankfully the strip windows in the saloon threw rectangular patterns of light across the expanse of deck. A hatch in the middle of the deck lay open. She waited for a lull between the swells, then raced across to it, dropping to her knees and clutching at the rim. Please, please, let him have gone down there and not over the side—because he sure wasn't anywhere else up here on deck.

She poked her head down into the gloom of the hatch.

"Ben?"

A groan answered her.

"Ben? Are you all right?"

Muffled sounds reached her, but no words. She sat back on her haunches. He was on board, that was the good news. She swallowed, her mouth dry suddenly, her breath feeling tighter in her chest. She didn't want to go down there. What if he was injured? She squeezed her eyes shut.

What if he was bleeding?

She felt the gorge rise in her throat and retched onto the deck. She kept her eyes focused on the dark tracks that ran between the deck planks. She had to go down there. She had to put her panic away and go and see if there was an injured man who needed her assistance. She was a doctor, for heaven's sake.

She squeezed the wet metal of the hatch for a few seconds longer, then nodded slowly. It was up to her. There was no one else. She started planning out the steps in her head. Planning was good. It calmed her. She'd check the numbers on the steering station, then she'd go down through the saloon, and then she was going to put on every damn light downstairs and open every door and calmly deal with whatever had to be dealt with.

She climbed to her feet and decided to ignore the trembling in her hands. A blast of salt-wet wind stung her face, and she paused to suck in a great lungful of it before making her way back to the cockpit.

The quiet inside was immense after the roar of the wind upstairs. She made her way forwards, bracing her hand on the back of a couch to keep her balance. She hadn't been forward of the saloon in the day and a half she'd spent on board. There were three doors there, so she opened them all and ran her hand around the insides of the doorways until she found their light switches. The first opened to a bathroom, the second a workroom piled high with canvas sacks and boxes. The third door opened up to a cabin, and lying on the floor of it was Ben.

As she entered, he raised dazed eyes to her. "Get my laptop."

She swallowed, trying to clear her head. Blood. Was there blood? She had to know. "Are you okay?"

Her voice sounded weak to her ears, like she was speaking through cotton wool.

She gave him a rapid once-over—the floor beneath him, the faded shorts he wore, the bare expanse of chest—his face was white, deathly so, but she couldn't see any blood. No spreading sticky blackness. She felt tears sting her eyes, tears of relief, and some of her tension dissipated.

"Laptop. Now," Ben growled, then sank his head back against the floorboards.

Sabrina reacted to his command without

thinking and spun around to fetch the laptop from the chart table. The moment in the saloon helped. She felt her breathing return to normal, some of her old competent self emerge.

"Not too injured to be cranky," she muttered. But still, his abrupt order was a good sign; it meant his brain was working. Her hands barely shook as she unplugged the laptop. And a good sign for her, too. Maybe she'd get through this.

"Open the lid," he said when she brought it back into the cabin.

The laptop hummed into life.

"Honey?" Ben all but barked the word. "What's our heading?"

"Currently 334 degrees, Ben, darling," the computer said.

He kept his eyes shut, but she heard his huff of breath. "Thank heaven for that. Sabrina, how are we steering?"

"I tied the wheel to the table."

There was a pause. "Good thinking. But go and untie it and Honey can put the autopilot on."

She frowned. "Okay. But what about you? Are you injured?"

Ben winced. "Boat first. Me second. Untie the rope."

Sabrina trotted back through the saloon and up to the cockpit and undid the rope. She watched as the wheel starting autocorrecting itself, and the direction on the compass settled into the correct heading. "Hmm," she sniffed. Honey knew her stuff.

She turned and headed back down to the front cabin. By the grim set of Ben's face, he'd done some sort of damage to himself when he'd fallen through the hatch. The steering crisis might be over, but her personal crisis was still careering way out of control.

He hadn't moved when she returned, but Honey was humming away beside him, and her screen was covered with dials and charts. Sabrina took the time to inspect him properly, then shot a look up to the hatch. It was a good seven-foot drop from the ceiling to the floor of the cabin.

"Ben?"

He opened his eyes and moved his head slightly. "I think I've broken my arm. If you can help me up, I've got a first aid kit in my cabin."

She dropped to her knees beside him, trying to ignore the up-down motion of the boat as it rode the swell. She ran her hands down his left arm, squeezing gently as she went. He didn't react; clearly it wasn't that one. His other side was wedged up against the foot of the bed. She hefted her arm into the crook between his good arm and his torso. "Try sit up now," she said.

Ben hissed and swore as she levered him up to a sitting position and pushed until his back rested against the bed. His eyes had glassed over, and a sweat had broken out on his forehead. His right arm lolled uselessly at his side, and its shoulder slumped forward unnaturally.

"It's not broken," she said matter-of-factly. "You've dislocated your shoulder."

"Hurts like a bitch."

"I bet. Lucky for you, I can help."

Ben's eyes snapped open and stared into hers. "Help how?"

Sabrina pursed her lips. This was the moment where she should tell him he could relax, she really could deal with his injury. Setting his shoulder would be a piece of cake, in fact, because she was so relieved he wasn't awash with blood that she felt euphoric. But it was the *what happened next* that had her hesitating. She would say she was a doctor. He would say what sort. She would say surgeon. Just thinking the word surgeon got her breath hitching and her pulse pounding.

No.

She couldn't do it.

She nodded at him, and mentally crossed her fingers for the lie she was about to tell. "I've got brothers. Common rugby injury." She smiled at him to reassure him. If she was calm about treating him, he would be calmer about letting her treat him. "If you played normal sports in America, you'd know the game I'm talking about."

She looked about the cabin. Other than the fact it was bouncing round like they were having this conversation in a bouncy-castle with a hundred sugar-fueled toddlers leaping about in there with them, it would do nicely. "We need to slide you up and backwards so you're lying on the bed."

Ben held her eyes with his. "Is this really going to work? Because if I'm not compos mentis, we are in deep trouble out here. You can't sail."

She held his good arm and gave him her most reassuring doctor look. "It's going to work."

With a sigh, Ben levered his feet under himself and pushed, while Sabrina held his limp arm.

"Wriggle up so just your knees and calves are off the bed," she said, and she climbed up behind his shoulders and hauled him as he shuffled backwards. He was heavier than he looked and warm. Very warm. His muscles bunched as he eased himself down, on his back, across the length of the bed.

"Hell," he said, breathing heavily. "What now?"

"Now you do nothing. Just lie there, try and relax if possible."

Sabrina stood up on the bed above him, with one foot on either side of his chest. His stomach was bare, its abdominal muscles ridged with pain. She dragged her eyes away, hoping he would blame her flushed cheeks on exertion rather than the very un-doctor-like feelings his bare torso was causing.

"Breathe in and out, deep and slow," she said, pressing her heels in to his sides to steady herself against the pitch of the yacht. The cabin ceiling brushed her head, but she was thankful for it. It gave her better purchase. Ben was a big guy—getting enough leverage to pop his arm back into its shoulder socket was not going to be easy.

"This might hurt a bit."

She bent down, lifted up his limp arm, and held his forearm firmly with both her hands. Then she worked the toes of her right foot into his armpit. "Ready?"

"Get it over with."

"On three," she said, then without stopping to count, she pulled with all her might on his dislocated arm.

He let out a bellow of pain, but she felt the pop as the ball of the bone slipped back into the socket, and gently released the pressure on his arm. Dropping to her knees beside him, she bent the arm at the elbow and ran her fingers up the humerus bone. It wasn't broken.

She let him have a few moments of silence. She needed a few herself. The crisis was over, but it didn't make her feel euphoric; it made her feel sick. Thankfully he hadn't injured himself even more, although, by all accounts, having a dislocated shoulder was enormously painful. Time to see if he was going to be okay. She mustered up a cheerfulness she was far from feeling.

"Was that a shriek I just heard?"

He opened his eyes, his green-blue gaze locking with hers. She could see the relief in them.

He raised an eyebrow. "Men don't shriek."

She stroked his wildly messy hair back from his face before she could stop herself. "I won't tell if you don't. How does it feel?"

He groaned. "Damned sore, but immeasurably better." He gave a short laugh. "Your brothers must run screaming from the room every time they see you if you've done that to them."

Sabrina dropped her eyes. The weight of the lie bothered her. "I get them to sign a waiver first." She changed subjects; it was easier than dwelling on her problems. "Okay, now we need ice. Pain meds. Triangle sling. You're going to need them."

He looked at her. "You know a lot about this."

She paused and considered what she was saying. "Well, that's what they always do after a dislocated shoulder," she said. At least, that's what she always prescribed after setting the dislocated shoulders of rugby players at St. Joseph's.

She relaxed, finally. Ben really did seem okay. She thought for a moment about the herd of noisy brothers she'd invented. Pity they weren't real. They might have directed some of her mother's ambition away from her and her sister.

"Where's your medical kit? Let's see what it's got."

Ben shook his head. "I need to get up top. We can get them on the way. Can you give me a hand?"

"Sure." She helped him into a sitting position, where he cradled his injured arm in front of him. "Ready to stand up?"

"I can do it."

She stayed kneeling on the bed as he made for the doorway, ready to jump off if he looked unsteady on his feet.

He turned at the door and looked at her, one long look that began as a thank you but shimmered into something that put a gallop into her bloodstream.

"You look good in a bed," he said.

And winked.

13

*B*en arched his back, trying to find a more comfortable position on the squabs. It was time for another batch of painkillers, but Sabrina had fallen asleep on the seat opposite his, and he didn't want to disturb her; she'd been up for most of the night. It'd be all hands on deck soon enough—all three of the hands on board that worked, that is.

He couldn't believe he'd been so dumb and distracted. His eyes rested on the sleeping form of his stowaway. She was a distraction all right, even fast asleep and rolled up in a blanket.

He looked up at the stars, at the spray of light running across the night sky. Not a cloud to be seen. Pablo's theory that giant sea turtles used the stars to navigate was a wonderful thought to hold in his head on such a beautiful night. He imagined the sea captains of two hundred years ago standing on the decks of their brigantines with their sextants, while beneath them in the warm waters of the Caribbean, sea turtles were popping their heads up from the swell to pinpoint the very same stars.

This was the glory of sailing, of living at the whim of the wind. He had time to let his thoughts fly in new directions...like in the direction of Sabrina. Was it just a few hours ago that he had kissed her in his galley kitchen?

She unsettled him. Her looks, sure, the woman was hot. But the nagging feeling remained that she was hiding something from him. Something big. But why? If she had stowed away on purpose on a lark, he could understand her being cagey, but that scenario just didn't ring true. For starters, she couldn't tell one end of his boat from the other. And she was no itinerant. She was educated, smart, resourceful...which begged the next question. Was she educated and smart enough to be an investigator, sent to worm her way into his life at the behest of the legal team in San Francisco who had slapped a lawsuit on him? That was the real question. He didn't trust coincidence. Which meant he couldn't trust Sabrina.

His laptop beeped gently on the cushion beside him, and he watched as a flurry of messages started scrolling over the screen. The internet was back up. The *Silver Girl* was close enough to land to reenter the real world. He ran his eye over the incoming emails. His father, friends, stock reports...he kept scrolling through until he reached the string of emails from his lawyer, then clicked on the top one and started reading.

I'VE DONE a bit of digging, Ben, and it seems there's another reason behind the buy-out company's pursuit of you. They've got finance trouble. They overstretched themselves when they bought your company, and now to help with the cashflow, they've laid off staff and compromised productivity. That's what's caused clients to jump ship, not any fictitious client poaching you have done. When I've finished compiling my report, I think we'll be able to scuttle their claims.

I found out a bit more about the investigative team they've unleashed. And we may have a problem. They've hired a shark of a woman—one of those "you eat what you kill" types—she's probably offered them a deal: her fees will be a cut of whatever juice she can squeeze out of you in a settlement to avoid a court case over breach of contract. Word is she's unethical. If she can't find proof, she might try and fabricate enough to make you settle just to get her out of your hair.

So watch your back, Ben. I'll be in touch when I've learned more.

HE SAT BACK TO THINK. It was bad enough that the buyers of his business were screwing it up for customers, but even more infuriating that they were willing to take potshots at him to get themselves out of their own financial hole.

He rubbed his jaw, then typed in a reply to his lawyer. *Send me a photo of their hotshot, will you? And anyone she might be employing to work the case.* He hovered the mouse over the *send* button for a second, and let his eyes drift back to his sleeping stowaway. The stowaway who had been snooping around his laptop.

"Hell," he muttered, then clicked *send*. He had to know.

SABRINA WOKE from a doze to find streaks of gray lightening the night sky. To their port side, a blue shadow loomed up from the sea to a high, mountainous ridge. Anguilla, she thought, and smiled. Who would have thought she'd be so knowledgeable of sailors' cant after an unplanned voyage at sea?

Port, starboard, mainsheet, jib. It had been an educational few days.

She eased her shoulders under the crackle of the waterproof jacket Ben had loaned her from his stash downstairs. Not that it had rained, but the wind had been high all through the night. It was cold on deck, and she had felt obliged to stay in the cockpit. Ben's face throughout the night had been a picture of fatigue.

She wondered if he'd had any sleep. His shoulder must be painful, even with the aid of the painkillers. And he'd have to be worried about sailing his boat. She was learning, but she was still more of a hindrance than a help on board. Honey had been in charge of steering through the long night passage, but with each major course correction, the sails had to be trimmed.

Ben was curled on the cushioned seating on one side of the wheel, and she was on the other. His back was propped up, and the triangle bandage she had used to secure his forearm to his chest was hidden under a quilt. His gaze was distant; he looked a million miles away. She wondered if he was brooding on the investigator he claimed was after him. Who he had accused her of being, about three seconds before he'd sent her into a head spin of need and heat with that kiss in the saloon.

She shook her head. She couldn't even investigate her own life at the moment, let alone embroil herself in the life drama of someone else. Even if that someone was as good a kisser as the handsome captain of the *Silver Girl*. She threw her blanket to the side and headed for the stairs. A shower. Coffee. She'd not be finding answers to any of the conundrums she faced without either of those.

Thirty minutes later, she felt like a new person. She flicked the gas light on under the kettle and hummed to herself as she bustled about in the kitchen. The ordinariness of the chores was settling. She loaded a tray with coffee cups and the blister pack of painkillers. Oranges hung in a mesh basket from a hook above the saloon table, so she sliced two into wedges and arranged them on a plate. What else? The pantry was loaded with pasta and rice, canned tomatoes and chili beans; her stomach balked at the idea of eating any of that for a dawn breakfast. A forage through the fridge was more propitious. She pulled out bread, eggs, and bacon. Hallelujah. Bacon and egg butties sounded perfect.

She added a pile of hot sandwiches to her tray, poured boiling water into the coffee mugs, then shrugged her way back into the jacket. She'd switched the sarong for her blue beach dress, thankfully dry and salt-free now, but its thin cotton was no match for the cool of the sea breeze. Gripping the tray, she made her way up the stairs to the cockpit, wedging her hip into the side of the handrail as she did so to help her keep her balance.

Ben saw her coming through the hatchway and stood up to close his good hand over her elbow to steady her against the buck of the boat. His eyes fastened on the loaded tray.

"Now I know how mermaids have been luring sailors to their deaths for centuries."

She sat the tray down on the cockpit table and slid round the other side of it to her cushioned seat, pulling the blanket back over her knees as she did so. "Oh really? And how's that?"

"Coffee. Bacon." He picked up the blister pack of drugs. "And painkillers."

Sabrina picked up a sandwich and sank her teeth into it. "Mmmf," she said.

She studied Ben as she ate. His stubble had grown in even further overnight, a dark-gold shadow over his jawline. Behind him, on the horizon where sea met sky, a blazing line of light heralded the imminent sunrise. The day was starting.

"How's the shoulder?"

He nodded. "I think I'm going to live."

She took a sip from her coffee, feeling the heat of it sink in. She imagined her caffeine-deprived synapses doing their happy dance; it wasn't a skim latte from a professional barista, but it wasn't bad.

She cast a glance about her, at the magnificent

yacht pushing through the swell, the countless acres of sky above them, its stars just starting to fade in the growing light, the giant sleeping island off the port bow looming larger with every mile they covered. She smiled. Not bad at all.

She couldn't remember the last time she'd had a picnic under the fading light of dawn stars. If she'd ever had such a thing. Her life in London had been structured towards ambition: striving at school to gain the marks necessary to enter a medical degree, striving at university to gain entry to a surgical specialty program, striving at home to uphold her mother's ideas of how her two daughters should look, act, be.

And the more her sister rebelled at the strictures of home, the more Sabrina had toed her mother's ruthless line.

The widow of a surgical legend, the man who had pioneered open-heart surgery before his untimely death years ago after a fall from a horse, Lady Susan Gray had embraced her new role as grieving widow after his death. From eulogist at the funeral to speech-giver at hospital fundraisers, she used each new role she was offered as a stepping-stone. Fundraising committees had bloomed under her stewardship, and her most recent move had seen her take up a position on the board of St. Joseph's Hospital, the very hospital at which Sabrina worked.

Well. Used to work. Before the Gray family imploded with her sister's suicide and she lost her nerve.

She let out a long sigh and let the ocean breeze running over her face soothe her. Maybe the truth was that she would never be able to operate again. Maybe that was why she was having such a hard time accepting it. The path she had laid out for her life had broken, and she no longer knew where it was safe for her to place her feet.

A warm leg slid against hers under the table and stayed there.

"You look...worried. What's up?"

Sabrina set down her coffee cup and dragged her thoughts away from her problems. For once, it wasn't difficult. Her thoughts had all leaped, of their own accord, straight out of her brain and rocketed down her torso to her right leg where the rough-haired calf of the man in front of her was pressing.

It's just skin, her rational self tried to whisper. Cells and dermis and tissue and hair follicles. But her other self wasn't listening. She cleared her throat, strangely loath to bring the contact to an end, and prevaricated.

"Not worried, exactly. I was just wondering how we're going to bring the sails down when we get close to wherever it is we're going."

"Mmm. I've been giving that some thought." Ben

quirked an eyebrow at her, and at the same time she felt a toe, or toes, brush over her foot.

She pursed her lips. Was that an accident or on purpose? She decided to leave her foot where it was. "And?"

"Pablo's turtle project is on one of a pair of coral cays just beyond the northern tip of Anguilla." He pointed to the horizon ahead of them, where the mountains of the big island dropped down to a deep blue horizon.

"There's a dock there, a timber jetty we can tie up to." He glanced at his watch. "I've sent Pablo a message, asked him to have one of his volunteers bring him out to us in his workboat, so he can come on board and help us drop the sails."

Sabrina nodded. It was a good plan. She opened her mouth to ask about phone reception but then huffed in a breath as she felt the hot pressure on her foot increase. Oh, that was definitely on purpose.

It was her turn to quirk an eyebrow. "Are you playing footsie with me?"

He gave a lopsided grin. "Must be the painkillers. My defenses are down."

Sabrina smirked and brought her feet up so she was cross-legged on the seat, facing him over the varnished table.

"What a shame. I've just recharged on caffeine. My defenses are way up."

She put her elbows on the table, resting her chin on her hands as she perused him. "So," she said.

He sat up on his side of the table, his bandaged arm across his chest, his other coming forward to lie on the table between them. "So?"

"So here we are. The journey's nearly over."

She ran her eyes down his face, his raw good looks made even more appealing by his wind-tumbled hair and the scruff on his jawline. Her gaze was drawn, unwittingly, to his mouth, and her breath stalled as she remembered its blistering assault on her senses yesterday in the saloon. Was she really ready to say goodbye? Just when she was learning to say hello?

He reached his good arm down below the table and brought something out of his pocket. His phone. He placed it on the table between them and pushed it over to her.

"We've got reception," he said. "You're welcome to use it. It's your call."

She got the feeling he was talking about more than a telephone conversation. She prevaricated. "My friend Antonia might be wondering where I am," she said. "I don't want her to worry."

He nodded.

"And I need money. Identification. Clothes."

He moved his hand and captured hers, bringing

them down to lie on the table. He squeezed gently. "Clothes are overrated."

She felt her heartbeat kick up a notch. Would she regret it if she didn't stay around long enough to explore whatever it was that was building between them? This unlooked-for heat that was beyond her experience?

"Maybe Antonia could send me a few things." The words slipped out before she had time to edit them in her head. Before she remembered he didn't trust her and had issues of his own, issues she was in no position to be getting involved in. Before she remembered she had issues of her own, and her issues were moon-sized. They eclipsed any chance she had of feeling the sun.

She backtracked. "But of course, I could just be masquerading as an accidental tourist while I flush out your inner secrets for my evil employer. How many pancakes you eat in one sitting. Why you're having a slightly creepy robot-romance with a laptop called Honey. That sort of thing."

Ben chuckled. "I can compartmentalize. I can wonder cynically about Sabrina the secret-keeper at the same time as I'm kissing Sabrina the bewitching. How about you?" He pulled on her hands, encouraging her to shift around on the seating to his side. "Come closer."

Her brain scrambled. She was bewitching? That

didn't sound right. But she certainly felt bewitched as she moved around the cushioned seating until she was side by side with Ben. Her blanket had slipped off, and she slid under his, feeling the warm cocoon of air rising from his body envelop her. His good arm curled her in close, and she closed her eyes on a groan as his lips came down on hers.

Her senses imploded, and she twisted on her knees, running her hands up his neck to grip his hair. He broke away to press his hot mouth against her neck, and she arched her back, pushing into him. Her fingers skittered down over his shoulder and ran into the twist of the triangle bandage. She fought through the fog of pleasure to get words out.

"Don't hurt your shoulder."

"To hell with my shoulder."

His good arm reached up under her jacket and tried to push it down her arms. She shrugged out of it, her back pressed against the table, her knees somehow straddling his, and heard it fall behind her in a clatter of mugs and breakfast dishes. She ignored it all, too intent on the lips that were running a hot current of electricity down her collarbone, the busy hand pushing at the straps of her beach dress. She felt cool air and gasped as her dress fluttered down to her waist. Ben's arm wrapped around her hips, pulling her up so she rose on her knees, and his hot tongue traced the swell of flesh that flowed, milky-smooth, from her bikini top. She made breathy sounds of encouragement, barely thinking, barely breathing, and when his busy mouth closed over her, she shuddered.

She kept one hand in his hair, holding him close, and ran her other hand up the warm curve of his bicep, squeezing at muscle and sun-browned skin, running her hand in under the soft fabric of the sleeve, thinking she'd have to rip it off him any second now before her need exploded, before her—

"Hola mis amigos. Bienvenidos a Anguilla."

Sabrina froze, her hair a wild mane, her dress at her waist, her breast heavy in Ben's hand. She was dimly aware of a voice shouting from behind the stern of the yacht, of Ben pulling away and straightening her clothing, then getting to his feet. Her lips throbbed. Her pulse raced. She felt giddy and full and mightily frustrated all at the same time. She raised shaking hands to her hair and smoothed it before somehow standing, dazed, her hands braced on the table.

Ben was at the wheel, turning the *Silver Girl* so she faced the breeze. Sabrina could feel their speed slowing, and the sails started to flog as the push of wind spilled from them. The sound slapped at her heightened senses, and she met Ben's eyes for one blazing moment of need before he looked away to the ocean behind them.

She followed his gaze. A scrappy looking boat, more dents and scratches than timber, bobbed in their wake, twin lines of foam spinning out from its outboard motors. A driver hunched behind a small windscreen, and standing on the bow was a huge man, hair waving in mad dreadlocks about his face, grinning up at them and flailing his arms like an airport worker bringing a jumbo jet in to land.

Ben's friend, Pablo, had arrived.

14

Sabrina's breath caught as the *Silver Girl* motored around the headland and the sheltered cove of the Manatee Cays stretched out before her. A gentle hill, densely green, rolled down to an expanse of white sand, blinding in the early morning light. The water was smooth, clear; its patterns of aqua and indigo and cobalt shimmered over the sand. Reef was clearly visible off the point, and brain coral outcrops pushed almost to the surface, their soft corals waving in the clear water. Beyond the reef, over a rough stretch of rock-strewn water, lay a smaller coral cay.

"It's pretty shallow," she called warningly to Ben, who was at the wheel, his eyes flicking between the instruments on the helm and the water beside the boat.

"There's a channel, we're fine."

A warm hand patted her on the back. "Girl, all is good."

She smiled at Pablo, who had clambered aboard to help Ben stow the sails. "Your island is breathtaking."

He winked. "Wait until you meet my Maggie."

A bleached timber dock pushed out from the sand of the cove, and a cluster of people gathered there. The *Silver Girl's* motors dropped a note, and the boat slowed, then slid smoothly up to the dock.

The next minutes passed in a blur of organized chaos. Fat white fenders were tossed between the boat and the dock and tied off around stanchions; ropes were wound around bollards; a small army of barefooted, cutoff-denim-wearing young people poured aboard and dived downstairs, bringing up boxes, sacks, crates, bags. Sabrina kept out of the way, bemused, wondering why a few days at sea had made her surprised by activity. It was not as though she wasn't used to managing a frenetic pace herself, in the surgical theater in particular. Perhaps sailing had provided some sort of catharsis to her turbulent mind. She felt rested, despite the conditions under which she had found herself aboard.

A woman was smiling at her from the dock, a cotton dress fluttering about her, its loose folds doing nothing to hide a heavily pregnant belly. Sabrina edged her way through the cluster of bodies on deck, aware of their curious looks, stepped through the section of rail that had been clipped back, and down to the timber box that acted as a step from the yacht to the dock.

Warm hands clasped hers, and a quizzical look welcomed her with frank brown eyes under a mane of red curls. "I am agog with curiosity. Hello. I'm Maggie."

She felt a little wrong-footed, unsure of her right to a welcome, and startled by Maggie's thick Irish brogue. "Sabrina."

"Sabrina? Oh, what a lovely name. I can stop referring to you as Ben's mysterious stowaway."

Maggie tucked a hand under her arm and led her away from the boat. "Let's get out of this wicked sun and in to the house for a cup of tea. You can tell me all about it."

She allowed herself to be led away down the dock to the beach. Her balance was a little awry after three days afloat; the land felt more solid than when she'd last stepped on it. She cast a look over her shoulder. Ben was on the deck, a canvas sack hefted up in his good arm, laughing at something Pablo had said to him. She felt something stir right up under her rib cage. a longing. For what, she wasn't quite sure. For the peace she'd found on the ocean, perhaps, the respite of a few days pretending to be someone she was not. Or maybe it was for the heat she'd found with her handsome captain.

She stalled. "Maybe I should stay and help."

Maggie dragged her away. "You can help me up at the house. Supply day is party day out here on the project. We've got jobs to do that don't involve lugging sacks." She shot a glance down at her swelling stomach. "I'm lugging around enough, I can tell you."

Sabrina allowed herself to be persuaded. She was an interloper here, and Pablo's wife was being so welcoming. She felt a silly rush of emotion at the ease with which Maggie had accepted her, a stranger. Keeping pace with Maggie, she made her way up a sand track to a low-set timber building nestled among the mauby bark trees. An open-air shed ran down the far side of a small clearing, filled with crates, buoys, scuba gear, ropes. Canvas awnings covered tents pitched on the grass, and in the center of the clearing was an outdoor fire pit lined with stones and shells, a grill perched above it. Swimsuits and towels and sarongs of every color were pinned to lines, hung over bushes, draped over the balcony rails. Maggie ignored it all and led her up into the house and through to a large wide kitchen that opened out onto a veranda. The cove lay before them, the blues of its waters shimmering in the sun.

"Sit," Maggie said, pushing Sabrina into a chair at the kitchen table, and swept aside a pile of charts and journals that covered the scarred worktop. She lit a match and waved it under the kettle until the gas caught, then turned and gathered cups from the draining board.

"Coffee? Tea? And the hungry hordes didn't quite finish off yesterday's cake." She collected a battered tin from the counter and set it on the table before them, levering off the lid to reveal a wedge of dark cake oozing with caramel icing. "Are you hungry?"

Sabrina smiled and shook her head. "I'd love a cup of tea. No food, really, we had a big breakfast. I can make it; I'm sure you have enough to do, Maggie, without waiting on some stranger who's just floated onto your doorstep."

"Nonsense." Maggie bustled about filling the teapot, then tucked a lopsided crocheted owl over the lid and spout. She settled into the chair opposite Sabrina's with a groan and fixed her with a stare. "Besides. Me making you a cup of tea is just a ruse. Now spill. Three days on the *Silver Girl* alone with our handsome Ben." Maggie mimed fanning her face as though she had suddenly overheated. "Don't leave out a single detail."

Sabrina blushed. "It's not quite like that." Then

she thought about where their morning romp may have ended up if Pablo's arrival hadn't interrupted them and felt her cheeks growing even warmer. "I didn't actually stow away on board. I had an accident."

Maggie sliced herself a generous serving of cake and licked icing from her thumb. "How thrilling. Start from the beginning," she said.

BEN GRABBED a couple of tablets and accepted the bottle of water Pablo was holding out.

"How is your shoulder?"

He rubbed his other hand over the offending body part. "It's been better, that's for sure. But I think it's improving. I'm going to have to get some help installing the camera equipment, though. They're fiddly beasts, and I might not have enough hands to get them working." He waggled the fingers that stuck out below the triangle bandage.

"You are in luck, my friend. Veronica is here for a few more days. She knows more about wires and gadgets than even you."

Ben gave him a punch. "Thanks, man."

"The tide is high now. I don't want to push you if you're not up to it, but if we can get the gear over to the western cay while the reef is under water, it will be a good start."

He nodded. "No problem. Come down into the saloon and we'll make a plan."

Pablo followed him down into the cool interior of the *Silver Girl,* and Ben lifted the lid on Honey to fire her up. "How's the internet?"

"Patchy, my friend. As always. If you're looking for the news reports of the *hueveros*, start your search in Ile Tintamarre."

"Honey, search for news reports and police reports from the last five days to do with turtle nests on Saint Martin and surrounding islands."

"Searching, Ben, darling. Results are onscreen now."

Pablo grinned. "Good to hear your voice, Honey."

Ben shook his head. "You know Honey's not actually a person, right, Pablo?"

The laptop bleeped. "So rude," said Honey.

He ignored the interruption and ran his eyes down the article. "You're right to be worried. Witnesses report a number of armed men in a high-speed vessel. I know turtle eggs are valuable, but you wouldn't think they'd generate enough income to interest professional criminals like these guys appear to be. They sound more like drug runners than *hueveros*."

"It might not be the money that is of primary

interest to them. There are people here among the islands who resent the conservation movement. Turtle eggs are a traditional food for the people; to have that tradition made illegal by the British, or the Americans, damages the pride of some local groups." Pablo shook his head. "I do not know for sure. But whatever their motives, I cannot risk the students becoming caught up with these criminals."

Ben finished reading the news reports. "We'll get the cameras up today."

Pablo nodded. "I'll have the gear loaded into the dinghy, then we can tow the double kayak over to the reef edge. Veronica can paddle you in over the reef."

Ben glanced back at the laptop as Honey reported he had fifty-three emails that needed attending to. "There's a crate in the storage locker under the table on deck. Can you put that in the dinghy too?"

"No problem."

Pablo eased his large frame out from the berth behind the saloon table. "And when you're done with the cameras, we can have a beer and you can tell me what's going on with you and that fine-looking stow-away you've brought with you."

Ben grinned at him. "My friend, if I knew, I'd tell you."

He turned back to his laptop, thoughts of Sabrina hot on his mind while he flicked through the daunting list of emails awaiting his attention. He flicked off a few quick responses, ignored others, then hesitated before tapping open the first of a series from his lawyer. Did he really believe Sabrina was some sort of spy, paid to infiltrate his activities and determine if he was breaking his restraint of trade contract? He shook his head. His gut was telling him no way.

What were the facts? The buyers of his business had clearly screwed up at management level, compromising their customer base. In security, your reputation and your speed of response to new threats was everything. They hadn't been up to it, they had lost business, and they were shooting at the stars if they thought he was somehow responsible for that.

If the buyers' lawyers were trying to claw back some money by threatening him, he figured he could just ride it out. He hadn't broken his restraint of trade agreement. And in a matter of days, his twelve-month freeze on working in internet security would be over.

He opened his lawyer's emails and started working his way through them. His fingers on the mousepad paused as he scrolled down to the photo of the investigator working on his case. A stern-faced young woman stared back at him, as unlike Sabrina as he could imagine a person looking. She could have been Pablo's younger, crankier sister. He let out a breath he hadn't been aware he was holding, then looked at his watch. Work now. Play later. And man, he was looking forward to that play.

"Honey. How's your battery?"

"Fine and dandy, Ben, darling. How's yours?"

He was really going to have to think about rewriting Honey's response algorithms.

15

Sabrina's fingers hovered over the keyboard, her thoughts flashing back to Ben's laptop's warning call on the boat. "No password?"

"No. You're fine."

A cluster of college students worked in the open air shed. Some tapped away on the bank of computers strung in a line down the long central table, protected from the weather by roll-down plastic sheets. Others scrubbed dive gear. Pieces of an outboard motor were spread out over the far end of the table.

"Okay then," she muttered, and logged into her webmail account. She scrolled through the usual detritus filling up her inbox, clicked on one from Antonia, and grinned. Antonia beamed up at her onscreen in a series of selfies aboard a small plane, her pilot visible in every shot. Clearly, her friend had been too busy with her burgeoning romance to call in a missing person's unit.

Relieved, she started typing. *Looks like you're having a fabulous time. Turns out, I've been having a little adventure of my own.* She paused, wondering how to compress the events of the last few days into a few words. Falling into a boat. Sailing the Caribbean. Ben. She felt her cheeks warming just at the thought of typing his name into an email. She shook her head. She was starting to sound like a schoolgirl, even to herself.

She decided the story would come across better in person so finished her email. *I'm on a coral cay north of Anguilla, and I may stay a few more days. Love, Sabrina.*

There. It was done. She'd made a deviation from her plan, a whimsical one, one that had nothing to do with her career, her life goals, her mother. She took a breath. She'd stay for a few more days and see where all this rising tension with Ben was leading. She was on holiday, after all. Surely she could take a holiday from her own personality as well? Rules, routines, expectations: where had it all gotten her, really? Maybe if she hadn't been so focused on her rigid path through life, she'd have been more of a friend to her sister. Cassandra may have been able to come to her instead of taking that final, irrevocable step.

She pushed aside the dark thoughts. She was on holiday from them, too. Switching to a search engine, Sabrina found the contact details for the Jewel Resort Hotel in Ballena and dropped them a message. She would need housekeeping to pack her a parcel of belongings. Like underwear, she thought, peeking down her sundress to the bikini she had been washing out each night. Shoes. A hairbrush.

She interrupted the students once more. "If I need to have a parcel delivered, how would I go about it?"

"Have them address it to the post office at Hawk Bay, they hold packages for us. There's a marina, a tourist village and so on just six miles from here. Someone goes over in the dinghy most days. If the address is marked to the turtle project, then whoever clears the post will bring it back for you."

"Great. Thanks."

She tapped in a message to the hotel, along with a quick list, and asked them to send it urgently, then sat back. Okay. Once she had her passport, her wallet, and her phone, she would feel less of an imposition on her hosts. She hoped having her belongings wouldn't turn her back into sensible and boring Sabrina Gray. She rather liked this new

Sabrina, the sailor girl who kissed handsome men at sunrise.

The computer gave a tinny ding and she saw a mail icon flash up on the screen. She clicked back into her inbox, expecting to see a reply from Antonia, who kept her phone on a very short leash. But it wasn't from Antonia. Sighing, she clicked into the message from her mother.

DEAR SABRINA

Dr. Ahnoud tells me you've cancelled your counselling sessions and have taken leave from the hospital. And without telling me! I am wondering if you have also taken leave of your senses. Enough is enough, Sabrina. Running away from the disgrace your sister has brought on the family is not the answer. And—you may have forgotten but I certainly have not—you promised to help me organize the hospital fundraising ball, so I will take this opportunity to remind you it is two weeks away. And I've already heard Maurice and Joan are attending with their son Sebastian. You remember him. He's just gone into private practice. Joan tells me he is quite the catch. I will expect to see you frocked up and ready to network. One does not rise through the ranks in one's career by indulging in escapades to the Caribbean.

· · ·

SHE HAD READ ENOUGH. She shot the mouse up the screen until it hovered over the delete icon, then clicked. Her mother was nothing if not predictable. Not a word of understanding. Not a mention of Cassandra, just "the disgrace". Her mother's email was the usual push of ambition.

Sabrina had made a mistake when she'd accepted a position at the same hospital her father had worked in before his death and where her mother sat on the board. She sighed. She had made a lot of mistakes. Not spending enough time with her sister, not being there for her, not seeing how desperate Cassie had become...

The sound of a bird chirruping in the trees interrupted her black thoughts, and she swung back on the stool, needing to be distracted. She took stock of the calm, orderly activity going on about her. Now was not the time for her to be idle; she'd just dwell on her mother's words and her own failings. And maybe she'd feel less like an imposition if she lent a hand. She stood up and walked the length of the shed, running her eye over the corkboards hung with notices, the pin-charts and machines. The resonant thump of a generator could be heard over the wind in the coastal scrub.

Pablo was seated on an upturned fuel drum, his chest bare, his mane of dreadlocks tied back in a gaudy banana-yellow bandanna. She sat on the grass next to him and leaned back against the timber post of the shed.

"What exactly do you do here?"

Pablo looked up from the wires he was soldering to a small transmitter and flashed her a grin. "Our English rose. Hello again."

He put a metal alligator clip into his mouth so he could use both hands and talked around it. "Have you heard of the Anguilla National Trust?"

Sabrina shook her head. "No."

"What about the Fauna and Flora International's Flagship Species Fund?"

"Sorry. No again."

One of the American college students caught her eye and winked. Mickey? Dan? She'd been introduced to them all, but the names had blurred.

"Not everyone's an activist, Pablo," the student said, grinning, before diving back into whatever was claiming his attention on his laptop.

Pablo started threading wire through the alligator clip. "You know turtles are endangered, particularly here in the Caribbean?"

She nodded. "That I know."

"Okay. Well, it is simple. We have a grant from the Anguilla National Trust. During the nesting and hatching season, we monitor the nests and protect them from predators. In the off-season, we explore the seas about Anguilla to identify the foraging areas for the turtles, so they can become protected sites, and we raise public awareness."

"It sounds fascinating. And we're in the hatching season now?"

"It's a little early for hatching, but the turtles are nesting." Pablo eyed her over the jumble of wire and tools spread before him. "I'm going to inspect the sites on the other side of the island. Would you like to come?"

"I'd love to. Now?"

"Yes, little rose." Pablo grinned. "Now."

He grabbed a hat from the jumble of gear in a crate on the counter and tossed it to her. "You'll need this." He led her to a battered jalopy with no roof: just four wheels, two seats, and a cargo tray in back. "Jump in."

Sabrina settled herself in the front seat, wincing a little as her bare shoulders came in contact with the sun-hot vinyl. The jalopy lurched forward with a crunch of gears, and they set off down a sandy track through dense clusters of prickly pear. She kept a hand on her hat as the breeze whipped at her hair.

"We have three turtles here in Anguilla," Pablo shouted over the whine of the engine as they turned onto a track that wound along the coastline. "Green, hawksbill, leatherback. They are all endangered. We monitor their nests here on the eastern Manatee Cay and over there on the western cay."

Sabrina stared over the narrow passage to the wilder, western island that Pablo was pointing to. She could see figures moving about on the shoreline, and a bright orange kayak pulled in above the tideline. "Are they your people over there?"

Pablo smiled. "That is Ben. And Veronica. She is a marine biology major, but she has an interest in electronics, so she has gone to help Ben set up the equipment he has brought over."

"The surveillance cameras?"

"Mmm. He is setting up his cameras to record what they see, but also we are trying to send their signal over here to our work shed so we can see a live transmission of the turtle nests on the western cay. Crossing the channel is not easy at night, so the volunteers usually camp over there when we have nests to monitor, but we don't have enough people to man all the nests. That is not the big problem, however."

Sabrina braced her hand against the door as they bounced through a rain-soaked ditch.

"The big problem is the *hueveros*."

"I don't know that word. Is it Spanish? Creole?"

"It is what we call the egg stealers. There have been reports on the mainland, and other isolated sites like ours, that there is a *hueveros* gang raiding nests to sell the eggs. It is a profitable business. The eggs are prized for food, and many Caribbean people feel it is okay for them to eat the eggs, as it is a custom going back many generations."

Sabrina stared over the water at the two distant figures working on the western cay. Now she understood the urgency. "Ben's arm must be mending miraculously well if he can use a kayak."

Pablo grinned. "It is a two-seater. Veronica did the paddling. It is not so easy to access the smaller island, as the reef runs to the shore. On a high tide, we can take the small dinghy in if we need to unload bulky equipment, like the sleeping tents, but the easiest way is to kayak. Veronica has had plenty of practice. We had a volunteer last summer who brought with her a stand-up paddleboard; she would glide over the water to inspect the nests and glide back fearlessly. It worried me a little. The current is swift in the passage when the tide changes. I insisted she have a friend in a kayak with a radio. I would not have liked to call her parents and tell them their daughter had drifted off on her longboard to Cuba, or Florida, or wherever the current might take her."

She smiled, a little. "My sister was like that. Fearless. Reckless, some would say. Impatient with anyone who tried to interfere."

"Was? She has grown out of such ways?"

Pablo was braking the vehicle, pulling it to a stop near a section of beach marked off with stakes and colored tape that fluttered in the breeze. He switched off the engine and looked across at her, his brown face shining in the heat of the afternoon.

"She died."

"I'm sorry."

Sabrina found herself engulfed in a hug, Pablo's wave of dreadlocked hair falling behind her head like a curtain. She heard its colored beads clicking faintly as they settled about her. A warm hand patted her back, and she felt overwhelmed suddenly...with his kindness, with her pent-up sadness and regret.

She smiled at him a little weepily as he eased back into his seat. "Thank you. It's not been very long, and I'm not dealing with it very well."

He nodded. "Grief finds its own way to unravel, Sabrina. At least, that is what I have found." He pointed ahead at a tumbled area of sand. "Oh, look. I think we have a new nest. Come."

He jumped from the jalopy and moved up the shore in long strides, and Sabrina hurried after him, dropping to her knees when he crouched beside the disturbed sand.

"How do you know it's a nest?"

"See the patterns in the sand above the tideline? The flippers spray the surface sand far to the sides, and on the return to the water, the turtle's tail makes this furrow. The turtles can be cunning and lay false tracks though." Pablo ran his fingers through a deep groove etched into the sand and crushed shells. "Let's make sure."

He dug carefully through the disturbed sand with his hands, and Sabrina leaned forward to help, scooping carefully and piling the sand to one side as Pablo was doing.

"We look quickly to make sure there are eggs, then we must cover them. Too much exposure to the air will change the temperature of the nest. If the eggs are here, then we add the site to our monitoring program." As he spoke, he paused and fluffed sand from an egg. He looked up and grinned at Sabrina. "I always feel like a proud father when I find one."

He held it out. "Cup your hand."

Sabrina did as she was told and held the egg gently in her palm. It was grayish white, slightly larger than a ping pong ball. A dimple creased it, marring the spherical shape. "Oh no. It's damaged."

"No, girl. The eggs all have little grooves, some large, some small. Like a thumbprint."

He returned the egg to the sand and began pulling the sand back over the clutch. "We will have good news to report back to the camp. Come. We have more nests to check."

The sun was throwing golden shadows when Pablo brought the jalopy back into the clearing in a spray of sand. Someone was playing music, a smooth reggae beat, and a fire had been lit in a huge fuel drum that had been split through the middle and laid on its side. Two of the college students were lying in a hammock sharing a beer, and a table had been set up on the grass with a bright tablecloth and piles of plates.

"Looks like your workday is over, Pablo," she said, eyeing the preparations.

He grinned. "Ben has brought us plenty of work in all those boxes and crates we unloaded this morning. Tonight, we relax. Tomorrow, we work. Come, my Maggie will want to see you before the party."

"Sabrina." Mickey, one of the students, was holding up a parcel. "Picked this up at Hawk Bay this afternoon. From Ballena."

Sabrina gave a squeal of delight and ran over. "So quickly? I don't believe it." She grabbed the parcel from Mickey. "Thank you."

Pablo held out his hand. "Come, little rose. That was lucky. Ballena is only forty minutes on a plane, but the planes do not come every day. You see? Fortune is smiling on you."

Sabrina smiled up at him and felt the balm of a warm breeze on her back, the comfort of her own clean clothes in her arms, and the promise of a long evening around a campfire with Ben.

"I hope you're right."

16

*B*en let the music flow over him. He was tired. The dull ache in his arm had been dragging at him all day. He'd have been better advised leaving it to heal for a day or so rather than spending the day rigging electronics and being paddled about a rough seaway in a kayak, but he had seen through Pablo's veneer of welcome and bonhomie. His friend was truly worried.

Since he'd heard some of the egg thieves on the coast of the main island of Anguilla were carrying weapons, Pablo had been unwilling to let the volunteers camp out at night to observe the nests. No one was in any danger of forgetting about the young environmentalist who had been murdered at Costa Rica in 2013 while protecting turtle eggs from poachers.

No. Ben had needed to get the monitoring

cameras installed as soon as possible, so the remote sites could be monitored from the safety of the work shed and the volunteers at the other sites wouldn't have to be spread too thinly across the ground.

He pulled a beer from the cooler. The college kids had done a run to the marina early in the afternoon and stocked up on party supplies. Beer and ice and corn chips, from the look of the parcels they'd unloaded.

He cracked the lid and took a long pull, relishing the cold. It had been a hot day, and the heat wasn't over yet. He lowered the bottle and cast a glance about the clearing. He hadn't seen Sabrina since the morning, and he felt, oddly, like he was missing her.

He smiled at himself, recognizing how foolish he was being. But since he'd decided he'd been a total jerk by assuming she was some ruthless investigator hired by crooked lawyers, he was keen to get his eyes on her again. Hell. More than his eyes.

His gaze traveled along the clearing and stopped. He stared. His heart thumped heavily in his chest. He forgot about the beer in his hand, the ache in his shoulder.

Sabrina was standing on the shallow flight of stairs that led from the veranda to the grass. Light from the overhead bulb shone down on her in a soft pool. Her head was turned slightly, and she was looking back at Maggie, who stood on the veranda flapping a tea-towel at a large hen that had chosen to roost on the railing.

Oh boy.

He exhaled slowly. She looked breathtaking. Her hair was loose, brushed and shining, hanging in waves down her back. She was wearing a skirt. A short skirt, in some sort of fluttery fabric that swished about her hips. She'd found a T-shirt, but unlike the one of his she had borrowed, which had buried her like a nun's habit, this one was tight. A soft blue, it was the color of the evening sky above her.

She turned, and her eyes met his. She'd done something to her face. Girl things: eyeliner and mascara and he didn't know what else, but he knew it was making his heart stutter in his chest. She smiled and walked over to him, and he used the time it took her to cross the clearing to try and gather his wits.

"Hey."

"Hey."

She smelled divine. He smiled at her and wondered for a second if he was looking a little goofy, then decided he didn't care. "You look different."

She glanced down at herself. "I spoke to my hotel. A friend of mine is married to the owner, so the manager must have given me the VIP treatment and raced a bag of stuff I'd asked for to the airport. So" —she ran a hand down her clothes— "voila."

He swallowed. She even said it with a French accent. He felt his blood plummet from his brain to his groin and decided he'd better get the subject away from what Sabrina had decided to clasp about all those warm curves of hers before he disgraced himself in front of the whole crew of the turtle project.

He cleared his throat. "So, what have you been up to all day? I'm sorry I seem to have abandoned you as soon as the boat docked. I got a bit caught up."

She walked toward the camp chairs set up about the firepit, and he followed her, sinking onto an upturned metal bucket. She shrugged. "I had a pretty fun day. Pablo took me for a drive around to the far side of the cay. We discovered a new nest. Then I've been helping Maggie and Dan in the kitchen. I hope you're hungry. Maggie has enough food in there to feed every college student in America. Hey, where's your sling?"

Ben nodded his head in the direction of the length of rope strung between the work shed and mauby tree. "Drying. Don't worry, my shoulder's feeling much better."

"I think this dance is mine."

He looked up. Mickey, the environmental engineering student volunteering from Dallas, was holding out a hand to Sabrina. The dark was settling on the clearing, and little glass jars of citronella oil had been lit, their wicks flickering light and smoke into the air. There were ten volunteers at the project at any one time, and tonight they were all dancing about the clearing, the music having changed from reggae to salsa.

Sabrina threw Ben a look, part alarm, part laughter, and he waved her off, content to sit on his bucket and watch her being spun about in the grass by the college boy.

Mickey caught his eye over her shoulder, and Ben gave him a look, drawing a finger across his throat, indicating instant death should Mickey try a move. Mickey gave him a wink, then dropped Sabrina over his arm into a dip.

"Show-off," he muttered, then grinned. After the heat of this morning's breakfast tryst, he didn't think he had anything to worry about.

17

*S*abrina leaned back in her chair, a half-finished glass of wine in her hand. The stars were out, a bright swath of them, lighting the night sky. She felt relaxed. Happy, even. And it had been months since she had been able to say that.

The college students were dancing on the grass or sprawled in hammocks after gorging themselves on the feast that had been served. Maggie sat on Pablo's knee, his hands wrapped about her swollen belly. His face was almost hidden in the dark, but she could hear the deep rumble of his voice as he chatted with his wife.

She thought of the ball her mother wanted her to attend in London in two weeks' time. Gowns and diamonds. Tuxedoes and limousines. Her mother's mansion in Mayfair still boasted its Regency ballroom, and she was a regular host of the St. Joseph's Hospital annual ball. Raising funds was its official purpose, but Sabrina well knew her mother ran it to serve her own ends. It kept her mother firmly plugged into the power grid that was the hospital board.

She'd rather be here, barefoot and blingless on this cay of sand and palms, than making small talk in her mother's ballroom to the powerbrokers of London's medical elite. Her eyes locked with Ben's, who was lounging in a chair on the opposite side of the firepit. Oh yes. She'd much rather be here.

He raised an eyebrow at her. "You want to go for a walk?"

Sabrina stood up before her prudent self could intervene. Yes, she wanted to go for a walk. Yes, she wanted this feeling of hope, of happiness, to continue. And, yes, she knew that what Ben was offering could turn out to be a whole lot more than a walk.

She watched him stand and slide into the shadows in the direction of the track to the dock. He stood there, waiting for her to come to him, his hand outstretched.

Her breath hitched. She was a creature of rules, of procedures. She plotted out a goal, and she plodded along until she'd achieved it. But Ben had not been part of her life goal. She had no rules to follow, no guide but her heart. For a second, doubts assailed her, and she felt like a skier who'd lost her way on a difficult ski-run and found herself off-piste, flinging her way through trees and snowdrifts at a headlong pace and out of control. Scared.

But also thrilled. She reached out and slid her hand into Ben's, and the doubts vanished.

Warmth. Companionship without pity. And so much more than that. Exhilaration. She felt the thrill of it sliding up her skin from where their fingers joined. It heated her blood and caught at her breath. Her thoughts skittered, sending her doubts and worries into a faraway place that couldn't impact her present, her now.

Ben pulled on her hand, directing her down the track, and she settled into his side, their clasped hands between them. She felt a half-laugh bubbling up. This was really happening.

The sand was cool beneath her feet. Her sandals were back at the firepit, kicked off some time during the meal. The mauby barks gleamed by the path, the lichen on their limbs catching the moonlight. A breeze lifted her hair from her face, and as they neared the beach, the beat of waves on the outer reef could be heard. Its rhythm matched the wild thump of her heart.

"It's so beautiful here," she said, as they stepped

down through the tideline of shells and seed pods onto the denser sand by the water. "So different."

Ben kept walking down to the waterline, where the calm sea of the inner lagoon lapped at the sand. Her feet sank into its softness, and the water curled around her ankles, warm and inviting.

"Different from where? You know, I don't even know where you live," he said, matching his footsteps to hers, their walk along the sand barely more than a dawdle.

She braced herself. Was she ready? Was she ready to tell the truth about who she was to Ben? To herself? She imagined saying the words out loud. I used to be a surgeon but now I'm not. I used to be a sister but now I'm not. Now she didn't know who she was.

"Sabrina?" Ben was squeezing her hand.

"I live in London," she said. "I've always lived in London."

"And...you're single?"

She smiled. "I am most definitely single."

"And your brothers play rugby, that I do know."

She felt the ground beneath her feet subsiding. Not the actual ground—the sand and waves were swirling serenely in the incoming tide, impervious to the debacle her life had become—but her emotional ground was falling away. She had lied to Ben on the *Silver Girl* when she had relocated Ben's shoulder.

Lied, because she felt like a failure as a sister and as a doctor. She knew she had to step into that dark place and face her fears if she was ever going to move forward, but she was not ready. She felt panic rising at the thought. She wasn't ready to face her problems, so she turned to the strong source of comfort walking by her side. She needed to distract him from his line of questioning. She needed to distract herself.

Moonlight played over his features, highlighting the wind-ruffled blond hair, the glint of scruff growing through on his unshaven cheeks. She made a decision. She had run away to the Caribbean to escape. What greater escape could she have than to lose herself in the arms of a handsome man?

She moved to stand in front of him and placed her hand, tentatively, on his body, where the thrust of his rib gave way to the muscle of his stomach. "Are you going to grill me all night with questions? Or are you going to kiss me?"

Ben's lips cocked in a grin. "I love questions. And sooner or later you're going to have to answer a few."

He leaned down and pressed his mouth to the pulse point below her ear. The stubble of his face rasped against the soft flesh there, and Sabrina swallowed a gasp. Pinpricks of delight shot up her spine, scrambling her brain. She shivered and pressed her body closer into Ben's, feeling the hot, hard length of him from breast to thigh.

His voice was low in her ear. "Maybe you could ask me a few questions of your own."

But she was past thinking. Ben's hands were roaming down her sides, slipping between skin and fabric and feeling their way along her ribs, her spine, the undersides of her breasts. Her eyes caught his. She didn't have questions, not tonight.

Just needs.

Demands.

"Come closer," she said, wrapping her arms around his torso, pushing feverishly up at his shirt.

His grin was wolfish. "I'm pretty close now."

"Not close enough," Sabrina murmured, then reached up on her toes and fused her mouth to his.

Minutes passed. Long minutes, where her blood sang in her head and Ben's hands danced on her body and she realized she had finally discovered what kissing was all about. It was about more. Much, much more. She tore her mouth free.

"Let's go to the boat."

"Let's stay here," he said.

She muffled a laugh and wondered briefly if that third glass of wine had been one too many. "The boat," she said again, her head swaying back as his lips burned a line up the column of her throat. His hands were here, there, everywhere: on her clothes, under her skirt, across the smooth warmth of her stomach.

He grabbed her hand and broke into a run. "Okay, but I hope you can move fast. You know I ran track in college."

She was panting already, her bare feet sinking into the suck of soft sand at the water's edge as she flew along the beach beside him. "Hockey," she huffed. "And shuttlecock."

"Shuttlewhat?" He turned his face to hers as they raced along the beach, his expression a comic wonderland of disbelief, and she laughed, exultant. Was this what fun was? Because it sure as hell felt like it.

"It's a British thing."

The timber of the dock was rough after the sand, its planks weathered by too much sun and salt, and she slowed to a careful tiptoe on her bare feet until Ben swooped her up into his arms.

"Your shoulder," she gasped.

He grunted. "You are so right."

He rearranged her so she was flung over one shoulder, his good one, like a femme fatale being rescued from a burning building by a burly fire-fighter.

She liked it. She liked it a lot.

She ran her hands down the planes of his back,

feeling her way down muscle and spine until the rougher fabric of his shorts halted her exploration.

He made quick work of the box step onto the deck, quicker work still of the hatch and varnished steps down into the dark of the interior. Green lights blipped on the chart table as he veered past it, and he spun around so they faced the aft of the boat, the captain's quarters she had never been in.

"I'm powering up, Ben, darling," said Honey, her voice multiplied in stereo through the speakers scattered over the inner sanctum of the *Silver Girl*.

"Power down, Honey," Ben ordered, then slewed Sabrina round so she slithered, inch by slow inch, down his chest, down his thighs, until her bare toes touched the floor and she was held to him, breast to chest. The corridor pressed close about them, a narrow, varnished shaft leading from the main cabin to his quarters.

It was a threshold. Sabrina felt a rush of affection. He was giving her this moment. A foot more, into his cabin, and the threshold was going to be crossed. This was her Rubicon. She could disengage herself. She could be Dr. Sabrina Gray: prim, assured, conservative, a slave to her career and her mother's ambition, a victim of her grief and guilt about her sister Cassandra.

Or she could step twelve inches into a new life. A new way of being. Maybe some fun and adventure would squeeze out the bleakness that had overtaken her heart.

She looked up, and her gaze locked with Ben's. His hair was backlit by the low lighting in the main saloon, its golden strands standing wildly on end, either from the sea breeze or her fingers. His eyes blazed with intent. He looked like a seafarer. An adventurer. He looked like escape.

She blew out a long breath, then smiled. She might not be ready to face her demons, but she was ready to take a risk. She slid her hand down from the broad shoulder she had been clutching, down the length of torso that separated shoulder from belt. She grabbed his buckle, the same buckle she'd held all those days ago on the street outside her hotel. She tugged. Firmly. Then she led him through the doorway into his cabin.

18

Sabrina's fingers were tight on his belt, burning there, like a brand. He didn't fully understand the sum of her worries, but he knew he didn't mean to add to them. Not tonight. Tonight was about adventure, about setting forth into an unknown future together.

She smiled at him. There was a tentativeness to it that pulled at his heart. "So," she breathed. "Are we really doing this?"

He held her arm, grazed his thumb along the smooth skin of her wrist. "It's a yes from me," he said. "You want to talk instead, that's a yes from me, too." He understood she was worried. Grieving. Pablo had told him her sister had died recently. He didn't wonder that she hadn't told him. So far their relationship had been wholly taken up with accustoming themselves to this force of attraction that charged the air between them.

He was a computer programmer. He understood variables and if-thens and knew the straight route often wasn't the right direction to take. But life was more complicated than a software program, and so far he was only sure of one thing: Sabrina was as attuned to him as he was to her. He knew it the way he knew the feel of waves under his boat's hull. Elementally.

And if the first time they came together he didn't know the whole story? Well, that was her choice and it was okay with him. The soothing could come first. Trust would follow.

"I don't want to talk," she said.

The hatch in the ceiling stood ajar, and cool fingers of sea breeze lifted her hair. He slid his fingers into the black silk of it, pulled her close, and fastened his lips to hers. She was a drug, he thought. No, a wine. Alluring. Intoxicating. And he had to have more.

He felt her hands push up at his shirt as he feasted on her mouth, and he obliged her by lifting his arms, feeling the soft pull of his T-shirt sliding up and off and landing on the floor. His belt was next. For a woman who looked like a raven-haired mermaid, she had some power in her fingers. His belt was open, his shorts being shucked down his thighs before his brain could compute what was happening.

"Your turn," he muttered against her mouth and slid his hands up under her shirt, ruthlessly ripping it up so it flew off to join his own on the floor. Her bra was white. Utilitarian. Like nothing a mermaid would ever wear, he thought with a smile. Or indeed a slick city lawyer masquerading as a stowaway.

He choked down a grin; he'd have to share the joke with her later. Much later. When he could talk again. When he could think. He slid his fingers under the straps, pulling them down her arms, his eyes on the smooth swell of flesh that he slowly, inch by inch, uncovered.

"God," he breathed, feeling the hot kick of lust ignite his loins. His chivalric dreams of soothing his worried stowaway skittered away as his blood pressure leapt past boiling point.

She trembled. He could feel the quiver rippling through her as his busy hands worked at hooks and buttons, zips and elastic. Her skin was smooth, dips and hollows that reminded him of the first pull of tide on a calm sea, and he took his time learning it. His hands reached down, fastening on her backside, dragging her in against him so he could feel all those glorious curves pressed up against him.

She moaned, and he caught it with his mouth. "You want to say something?"

She shook her head, her heavy hair falling across her shoulders, his arms. "I can't think. I don't want to think."

He'd forgotten that there was so much to feel, so much to know when two bodies came together. Or maybe it was just her body. His knowing. "Don't think, then," he muttered. Because he sure as hell couldn't, not crushed up against her as he was, feeling every inch of her heat.

And then he was done with words. His hungry mouth busied itself on her flesh. There was nothing of chivalry in his embrace. He was wild. Seismic. His body was in charge now, not his mind, and it was setting its own pace.

His lips fastened greedily over her breast, but he barely heard the moan she gave. Her hand slid up his side, and he arched, pushing into her fingers until she gripped him, her nails flint-sparking tiny arcs of fire across his body, his sides, his thighs.

He needed to touch her everywhere, all at once. His hands raced over her curves, cupping the smooth skin of her thigh, pulling it up and over his and holding her there, writhing against the heat of him, for long seconds of promise of the plunge that was yet to come.

When the throbbing in his loins could take it no longer, he bundled her backwards onto the bed and stood over her, dizzy with longing. Her hair was a black halo, layered over the colored cotton of his sheets, her face a pale shadow in its midst. Her eyes blazed up at him, hot, sultry, expectant. She was all that he had dreamed. More than he could dream. Her pale breasts claimed his attention, and he leaned forward to cup one as he settled between her thighs.

"Christ, I want you," he breathed.

She smiled. His siren. His stowaway. His.

"Then take me."

ater. Water was everywhere. Dark, rushing torrents of it, filling the gutters, spilling up from the drains, racing over the dark cobblestones. Freezing rain pelted down from leaden skies, smashing against the windows of the taxi. The thump-thump of the windscreen wipers sounded overloud in the dank, heated interior of the car. The brake lights of impatient commuters cut through the rain and mist, red neon flashes underscoring how slow the traffic was traveling, when she needed to be moving fast. Cassandra needed her.

Sabrina's fingers fumbled on the inner handle of the taxi door. She could run from here. She thrust a twenty-pound note at the driver and flung open the door, taking advantage of the snarl of traffic to dodge between stalled cars until her feet hit the pavement.

Beneath her coat, she still wore her scrubs, and the sneakers she wore for a long day at the operating table would allow her to run down the pavement. She was only a block away from the basement flat Cassandra called home.

The dark had closed in early as it always did in winter, made worse by the violent rainstorm that was sweeping London, but as she turned the last corner she was assailed by a barrage of light. Blue and white strobes revolved urgently, punching through the sleet; the police car she had frantically called from the hospital had beaten her to the flat, and it hadn't come alone.

Three cars were slewed at angles, squat little metro cars that were always first to a scene. Police-women and policemen huddled in their greatcoats above the wrought iron rail that led down to Cassandra's flat, forming a broad-shouldered wall that blocked her view. Why were they just standing there? Why weren't they running down the stairs, breaking in the door, stopping Cassandra from picking up the knife?

The phone call had come at the end of her surgical list. She'd been gloved and gowned, closing up a line of stitches, the blood of the teenage boy who'd been slashed in the face by a bottle in a pub fight staining the arm of her gown. It had been a long day in the emergency room—Saturdays always were

—and she'd thought the surgical nurse was coming in to tell her to prepare for a new case when she'd seen the set look on Su-Lin's face.

"You've got a phone call, Dr. Gray."

She could remember feeling confused. Su-Lin was an experienced nurse; she'd never bother the surgical team with such a trivial matter as a phone call.

"I'm not finished. Take a message."

Su-Lin had leaned in, a whiff of milky tea and cookie still on her breath. "Dr. O'Mahoney is stepping in for you."

The nurse had hustled her out of the operating room, stripped the gloves and gown from her numb arms, thrust the phone into her hand. "It's your sister. It sounds urgent."

"Cassandra?"

She hadn't spoken to her sister in weeks. They had found little to say to each other since Cassandra had turned her back on their mother and moved in with the photographer who had given her a start in modelling. Their lifestyles had been too different. Sabrina worked, all the time, and Cassandra played. Bars, theater openings, fashion shows, parties: her sister enjoyed a dizzy rush of social engagements and an even dizzier rush of street drugs. It was the drugs that had driven the biggest wedge between them. The drugs that Cassandra had tried to steal from the hospital under the guise of visiting her sister.

She had tried to intervene, to talk her sister into reassessing her choices. Cassandra had refused to listen.

The voice on the phone was weak and indistinct. "I've done it, Sabrina."

"Cassandra? Done what? What have you done?"

"The pills never worked."

Her head was whirling with possibilities, none of them good.

"You're scaring me, Cassie. Where are you? I'm on my way."

She heard her sister start to giggle, an odd noise that ended on a sob.

"I'm cold," she heard her say. "I didn't know the knife would make me so cold."

And then the line had gone dead.

Her nightmares always brought her to this moment. But no matter how many times she had to relive seeing her sister's body, the outcome was always the same. The freezing rain tearing at her hair. The flashing lights. The wall of police.

Her chest heaving with exertion, Sabrina pushed past the police at the rail, ignoring their shouts of warning. In the courtyard below, a medic was working on a body that lay sprawled over the mosaic tiles. Black hair, so like her own, spread about the white-as-bone face of her sister staring up at her. A pool of blood spread even wider about the body.

This was the moment when Sabrina's life imploded.

Her sneakers clanged on the rungs of the stairs down to the courtyard, but halfway down, an iron hand clamped on her arm.

"You can't go down there, ma'am."

The policeman was big, and the strobe lights from his car were blinding in her eyes as she turned to shake him off.

"Let me go. Let me go. Let me go."

She was screaming now, crying, wailing, dropping to her knees.

The pressure on her arm increased, and she bucked to get out of the policeman's grip.

"Sabrina! Wake up."

She reared upwards, dragging in lungfuls of air. Light shone in her face, but it wasn't a strobe light, it was flickering in through the windows of the boat cabin she was in. A hand was holding her arm, but it wasn't a policeman, it was Ben. She struggled to make sense of where she was. Who she was.

"Ben," she said on a gasp, a riot of conflicting images skittering on her subconscious.

He loosened his grip on her arm and ran it up to her shoulder until he was holding her neck, gently, as though he held a wounded sparrow. "Sabrina. Hey. You're okay. You had a nightmare."

A thump sounded above their heads, and over the raw thumping of her heart she heard the thudding of feet. Flashlight flickered in the main saloon: someone was on board the boat.

"What's going on?" Her voice was shaky. "Why are there flashing lights?"

Ben gave her a quick squeeze. "Shit. Stay here. I'll find out."

He rose from the bed, grabbing a sarong from the back of the door and wrapping it around his hips. He headed out of the cabin and closed the door behind him. Sabrina waited until she heard its catch snick into place, then threw back the sheet and started scrabbling around to find her clothes.

Damn it, it was too dark to see where they'd been thrown. She found the light switch to the bathroom in the cabin and spied her underwear tossed over a chair, her skirt in a crumpled heap at the end of the bed. She rammed herself back into them as quickly as she could, then took a moment in the bathroom to stare at her reflection in the mirror. Dark eyes peered back at her. When would the nightmares stop, she thought, crumpling against the sink, feeling the tears of mingled frustration and grief welling up.

She should never have read that email from her mother. How far did she have to run to get away? She shook her head and splashed cold water over her face. She was a mess. She would always be a mess. Tears came, and she choked them back. Choked them down, deep, where they couldn't hurt her. She was so tired of hurting.

She heard the cabin door open again, and Ben was there, filling the space, his mouth drawn in a tight line.

She found her voice. "Was that Pablo? Has Maggie gone into labor?"

"I have to go over to the western cay. The monitors are working. There are men on the beach raiding the nests."

Sabrina frowned. It was too much to take in. Just too much. "Now?" Her voice still shook. "Isn't it dangerous getting over there? Aren't the men dangerous?"

Ben pulled off the sarong, oblivious to his nakedness, and began rifling through drawers looking for clothes. She watched him slide his way into cargo pants, wince his way into a T-shirt, dig out tennis shoes from a basket in his closet. She counted his tasks, concentrated on them. Her panic was simmering just below the surface, and she needed to keep it there, to get it to calm the hell down.

She squeezed hot tears back. How could she calm down? Her mind was still quivering from the raw pain of the nightmare, and her body was still brimming with the glory of the most nerve-jangling sex she'd ever experienced. Her heart was lurching with fear for Ben, but also with fright at what Ben might mean to her and worry at how she would cope with this, when her history told her she would not cope at all.

She hugged her arms about herself to still the trembling. "I wish you didn't have to go."

"I'm going with Pablo. Have you seen the guy? He's built like a supertanker. We'll be fine. And it's high tide, so we can get in on the powerboat."

"I should do something. What can I do?"

Ben stepped in close, crowding her in the doorway to the bathroom. "Wait for me. Because when I get back, you and I are going to have a talk."

He pulled her in for a brief, hard lover's kiss, then pulled back to look at her again. "Okay? Shit. You don't look okay." He smoothed her hair back from her face, ran his thumbs over the wetness that clung to her cheeks. Kissed the top of her head.

"I hate to leave you," he said.

Then he was gone.

20

*B*en jumped down into the dinghy and had barely placed his backside on the wooden plank seat when Pablo rammed his large fist down on the throttle and the boat roared away from the dock. The volunteer, Veronica, was hunched in the prow, a heavy-duty flashlight in her hands. She kept it focused on the white reflective channel markers which pointed to the gap through the reef they would need to use to leave the anchorage.

The night was black. Midnight had been and gone, and the stars that tracked through the northern sky were covered by clouds. Pablo slowed to make the turn through the reef edge, and once clear of its protection, the chop of the open ocean tossed the dinghy like a cork. Spray arced up over the sides, drenching them.

Ben leaned over to the dinghy's driving console, where Pablo was standing at the wheel, protected from the spray and wind by a sheet of hardened acrylic plastic, and yelled in his ear.

"Which alarm sounded?"

Pablo turned to him, his beaded dreadlocks flying in the wind. "The motion sensors went off first. Veronica had the transmitter with her in the workshop and heard the alarm. She checked the cameras you'd installed earlier, thinking maybe we had a new turtle coming up to lay eggs. But it was men. We saw men on the beach."

He swore. "I'm sorry. I had Honey powered down. I didn't get the alarm."

Pablo's teeth flashed in the dark. "Don't sweat it, my friend."

But he was sweating it. He was sweating about a lot of stuff, and it was hard to put in order the magnitude of stuff that was bothering him. Sabrina. Wow. His thoughts stalled there for a time, just drifted on a wave of images and sounds as he replayed those moments in his cabin. He'd never felt so utterly suffused with longing. So utterly shattered by pleasure. And to have that rosy, unspeakably epic afterglow destroyed by first her nightmare and then Pablo's urgent call for help—

Hell.

And she'd looked absolutely vulnerable when

he'd left her. Still crying, he was sure, from whatever had haunted her dreams. Her sister's death for sure.

A wash of salt spray dumped over him as Pablo hurtled the workboat sideways across the swell. He had to put his thoughts of Sabrina aside for now. But when he returned to the *Silver Girl*, he was going to have the truth from her. He'd coax it out of her, if need be. And he knew how she reacted to him. He'd get his answers; he'd make her trust him.

The chop between the two islands that made up the Manatee Cays was steep and thudded ominously under the racing hull of their boat. "How far off high tide are we?" he said.

Pablo looked at his watch, pressing the button to illuminate the digits. "It was full about thirty minutes ago. We'll need to be in and gone within the hour or we'll be trapped until the next tide. This boat's draft is too deep to get over the reef after that."

"Our *hueveros* must be running to the same timetable," Ben said grimly. "So what's our plan? Do we know how many are over there?"

"The footage was too indistinct in the dark. We saw maybe two pairs of legs. Our plan is ,at best, to scare them off. We are not equipped to catch thieves. If we can intervene, send them on the way, hopefully, the word will get around that we are monitoring our nests and they will think it is too difficult to bother coming to disturb us. We can notify the

National Trust, and they can get the authorities involved."

He nodded. The tide was still plenty high enough for the *hueveros* to get back in their boat and disappear.

"Veronica," Pablo shouted above the noise of the wind. "The cay should be at your nine o'clock. Keep the flashlight low and try and find where the waves are breaking."

She waved a hand in the air to let him know she'd heard.

Ben pulled out the headlamp he'd shoved in his pocket as he'd left the *Silver Girl* and put it on, careful not to blind Pablo with it as he did so. The big man was holding his handheld GPS unit. The channel between the two cays was shallow and riddled with reef; they would need to follow one of their previous approach angles if they didn't want to bottom out on coral, and the GPS unit would show them the exact angle to take to reach the narrow strip of beach they used to land.

"Ben, can you shine your light ahead of us? I am going to slow down. Even though the tide is up, there will be some large coral outcrops that we won't get over."

He stepped forward into the prow beside Veronica.

"You okay, Vee?" he asked, wedging himself in beside her so he could look down in the water.

She was looking forward, scanning the crests of the waves with the big flashlight, moving its beam in a slow arc.

"More than okay. I'm stoked. To think, if we hadn't rigged that equipment up over there, the first thing we'd know about these raids would be when we found a beachful of empty nests. This equipment has given these turtles a chance, Ben." She nudged him with her shoulder. "Those fuckers don't come in here and kill my baby turtles and get away with it."

He grinned. Veronica had the head of a rocket scientist and the heart of a vigilante. It had been Pablo's lucky day when she'd decided to volunteer her considerable talents to turtle conservation.

A flash of color emerged from the inky water ahead of them, and Ben raised his arm to Pablo, indicating he should go wide. The dinghy slowed to a crawl. They were right over the outer cay's fringing reef now, and it was a fifty-yard journey over it to get to the beach.

"Any sign of their boat?"

"No," said Veronica. "They must have landed on the far side. Engine noise carries at this time of night. I reckon they didn't want us hearing them from over on the inner cay. I don't see any flashlights moving either."

Pablo's voice was a low growl from behind the steering wheel. "And they won't be having to waste time searching for the nests, because we've got them all pegged out for them. They'll think they're at an all-you-can-steal buffet."

The strip of beach gleamed ahead of them, and Pablo cut the engine as the dinghy's aluminum hull dug into the soft sand.

"What if they're armed, like those *hueveros* we heard about in Ile Tintamarre?"

Veronica seemed to have lost some of her gung-ho attitude now that they were faced with the reality of the dark and quiet of the outer cay. Civilization was a long way away.

Ben threw his long legs over the side of the dinghy, reaching into the storage locker on the prow with his good arm to bring out the anchor and its heavy length of chain. He walked it up the beach and rammed its pick into the sand.

Pablo laid a hand on Veronica's. "Vee, you can come with us or mind the boat. It is your choice. But I do have a plan, okay? I have faced poachers before. We know this coral cay, we know the tracks to get us back and forth. We're going to quietly go have a look at what the *hueveros* are doing. If they're armed—and that's a big if; most of these poachers are just looking for a cache of traditional food; they're too poor to own weapons—then we do nothing. We creep back to our boat, we get the hell out of here, and we call the authorities on Anguilla."

Vee nodded. "Okay."

Pablo continued talking. "If they're not armed, then we go tell them to move on and we rescue any eggs that have been taken. Got it?"

"Got it."

Ben transferred his headlamp to his hand. "Which camera had the footage, Vee?"

"Up near nest twelve. We'll have to head into the bushes, then take the inland track around to the next cove if we don't want to be seen coming along the beach."

"Okay, let's do it."

Pablo took the lead. He was the one most familiar with the island. They kept their voices low and their flashlights aimed at their feet. Veronica had untied the bandanna she wore as a headband and fastened it over her flashlight to dull its beam, and Ben could hear her breathing behind him. The track was sand, and dry as bone; it squeaked slightly as their feet landed in it, each squeak sounding too loud in the tense silence. There was no breeze. The trade winds often died out in the hours before dawn, and tonight was no exception. They could not rely on the wind in the scrub to mask the sounds of their arrival.

After two hundred yards or so, Pablo held up an arm and they all stopped. He turned to them. "Turn your lights off. We'll creep like ghosts from here. I think we're close."

The darkness was absolute as they switched off their flashlights. Ben waited for his eyes to adjust, and as they did, trees and scrub-bush made shapes of themselves around him. Pablo's bulk blocked his view forward, so he inched ahead beside him, then froze. In the gloom ahead, perhaps thirty feet away, was a man holding some sort of camping lantern.

Ben blew out a breath. A poacher. He could hardly believe it. He knew the others had seen the *hueveros* on camera, but it still came as a shock. What on earth was he doing, running about an isolated coral cay after criminals? In the dark? He was a computer geek, not a superhero. He made a chopping motion with his hand to the others to silence them.

"A man," he whispered. "He's at the tree line, just above nest twelve. I can't see any others."

Veronica's voice was just breath in his ear. "I'll crawl forward and see, then come back to you."

He watched her disappear into the darkness ahead of him, then turned to look at Pablo. "I don't like this."

It was one thing installing security equipment and monitors so they'd know when poachers showed up. It was another thing entirely to be out at night, hunting them, with no backup from authorities.

A rustling of twigs had their heads spinning back towards the beach.

"It's me." Veronica's voice was barely a sound.

She stood up, walking towards them until she bumped into them. Her hand gripped Ben's arm, and he winced; she had Pablo held just as tightly with the other.

"Guys. We've got a big-as-shit problem. There's three more down at the nests. Number twelve is gone. I'm sorry, Pablo. They've looted it. They're into another one now, I think it's sixteen. And this guy just here? Like right here in back of us? He's carrying a gun bigger than a baseball bat. If they see us, we are in huge frigging trouble."

21

For an instant, time stopped. They looked at each other, three shadows in the almost black night, just the whites of their eyes shining, and the faint strip of reflective tape on Veronica's big flashlight.

Ben was the first to respond. "Pablo, you lead the way. Vee, you're in the middle, I'll bring up the rear. Back the way we came, and quickly."

He saw their nods and waited for them to clear the space in front of him before he risked a glance back at the sentry who stood guard with the gun. He shook his head. Pablo would be thinking what he was thinking, that this was a lot more than any of them had expected to be dealing with. Turtles were important, vitally so, but not more so than their college students. Than Maggie, in an advanced stage of pregnancy. And Sabrina, crying in his bathroom, in an advanced stage of not-coping.

His thoughts drifted to Sabrina as he crept back along the path after the others. Well. Sabrina's not-coping would end tonight. As soon as he was clear of this drama and the authorities had been notified to do what they could about the armed poachers in Anguilla waters, getting into Sabrina's headspace was going to be his number one priority. If she was hurting, he could help. If she was running away, then he could run away too, until such time as she was ready to face whatever it was she was running from.

Whatever it was, he was willing. Resourced. Able. He wasn't letting go of his stowaway now.

Pablo and Veronica had disappeared into the gloom ahead of him. He picked his way along the path, not risking turning on the flashlight in his hand. The scant cover of stars and moon was barely enough to see, but just as he was wondering if he should risk his flashlight, he heard a whispered conversation going on ahead of him and slowed his steps until he was sure it was his friends.

Pablo was angry, pointing his finger. "Veronica, no! It is too dangerous. I will not permit this."

"You can't stop me, Pablo. I'm not here to play at being a conservationist. I am a conservationist. I'm going to do what it takes to stop these poachers. It's my risk, and I'm taking it. If you're worried about your project, your responsibilities as leader, don't. I quit."

As Ben neared them, Veronica disappeared from sight into the scrub.

He looked at Pablo. "What the hell?"

His friend rubbed his hands on his face. "Ben. Vee has chosen tonight to go completely batshit crazy."

"Why? Where's she gone?"

"She's had a mad plan. She said you gave her the idea."

"What?"

"In the dinghy. Something about the *hueveros* being on the same timetable as us to get their boat out before the tide drops too low or they'll be trapped."

"Oh, I am not liking where this is going," said Ben.

"Uh-huh. She's gone to untie their anchor rope and drag their boat out into deep water so it floats off over the reef before they return to it. This way the *hueveros* will still be here when the police come."

Ben looked at Pablo. Sure, brilliant plan, but risky. Too risky for a college girl whose parents were counting on Pablo to get her home safe and sound for another semester cycling round campus, eating vegan muffins and dating unsuitable frat boys.

"We've got to follow her."

"She took the flashlight."

He lifted his hand and clicked on his headlamp. "We're good. You better lead the way; I've only been here in daylight." He handed over the flashlight.

Pablo grunted, looking down at his watch. "Time's passing. We've got to get Veronica, and be back on our boat in the next thirty minutes, or we'll all be trapped here. Three of us and a gang of armed thugs." He wrapped the flashlight strap around his thick wrist and sighed. "Ben, my friend. I'm getting too old for this."

Ben thought of the bed he'd left to come out here, the softness of Sabrina curled in under his arm, the quiet and the heat he had found with her. "You and me both."

They set off after Veronica through the scrub. There was no track here; Vee had taken off at right angles to the track they'd been on, heading to the ocean side of the cay. Ben could understand her logic: the poachers' boat hadn't been near their boat when they'd landed. There weren't that many places on this cay where a boat could beach, even at high tide. She must have had a good idea where to look.

The scrub and trees weren't dense—rainfall was too infrequent and the soil too poor to generate proper growth—but the limbs proved that the prickly pears were well named. They snagged at his shirt, snarled on his calves as he raced through the thickets in Pablo's wake. Surely it couldn't be far? The cay was less than a mile long and barely a quarter of a mile wide.

He nearly stumbled as he leapt through the last of the scrub. The cloud cover had thinned, and a strip of moon illuminated the windswept shore of the cay. Down the beach, a powerful-looking speedboat rode the rougher seas of the ocean-side on a short anchor. He could see Pablo running just ahead of him, the thin beam of the headlamp in his hand flickering over the sand. Of Veronica, he could see nothing.

He breathed in sharply. Was that movement? Two things caught his eye almost in the same moment. One was the bulk of a man, emerging from the cabin of the boat to stand, his silhouette erect, against the powerful outboard motors at the stern. In his hands was the unmistakable shape of a handgun.

The second was the flash of a powerful light— Veronica's flashlight—sliding low, beneath the water, under the gunnel of the poachers' boat. If her plan had been to untie the anchor rope, it had been thwarted by the fact the speedboat had not been anchored up on the beach, as Pablo's was. No, the poachers had left their boat floating in a few feet of water, its anchor submerged beneath its prow. Perhaps they had been unwilling to risk being stranded in a falling tide in an anchorage they did not know.

Did Veronica know there was a poacher on board the boat? Surely she didn't. He must have been inside the cabin when she crossed the beach. The risk of taking on an armed man out here, on an island many miles from help, was too crazy, even for an idealistic college student.

Did the poacher know Veronica was under the boat? If he'd been in the cabin when she arrived, he might not have seen her light. But he'd see it soon. It was flashing about under the boat like a disco strobe at a Berlin rave.

Hell.

Thank heaven for the waves on this side of the island. The rougher ocean swell crashed in on the reef fringing the shore, obliterating much of the sound that might have traveled to the boat. But the waves were the only thing in their favor.

Pablo might not have seen the man in the boat. The light from the small flashlight he carried would wreck his night vision. And worse, he was a big man running in slow motion, waving a light around. When the poacher saw him, as surely he would if he looked up, Pablo would be an easy a target.

Ben had to warn them. He took a breath, then started to run. He hadn't been joking when he'd boasted to Sabrina earlier that he ran track in college. He'd more than run track. He'd paid his way through college on a track-and-field scholarship. He'd owned the track back in the day. Of course, back in the day he hadn't been running along soft sand to save a foolhardy girl he barely knew from a criminal who was holding a gun. Back in the day, he'd also been about fifteen years younger.

But he put all that behind him as he worked himself into a sprint and floored it down the beach. His arms worked at his sides. His thighs were pistons charging up-down, up-down. He passed Pablo, called to him, warning him, relying on the crashing waves to cover his noise from traveling too far.

"Gun! Gun. Careful. Gun."

He wasn't going to make it. Veronica was thigh deep, her flashlight raised high; he could see her panning through the water, looking for the anchor rope so she could slip the boat from its chain, but the man with the gun had seen her. He was stalking her from the deck of the boat. What were his thoughts? What did he plan to do? Surely they had researched the turtle site. The *hueveros* must know that a team of researchers and science students monitored these nests.

The combinations and permutations fluttered through Ben's brain as he ran. Algorithms were his thing, after all. They were how he'd made his internet business leader of its pack. He made himself think like a criminal. What would the gunman do? Shoot her, then dump the body to get rid of the evidence? It would be easy enough out here to take the girl's dead body out wide, to the deep, where the incriminating bullet wound would never be found. She'd be one more statistic: one more lost swimmer in the Caribbean, lost in the pull of the tide.

Or maybe he'd just try and scare her off?

Ben couldn't risk it. She was a college student. And a brave one. He couldn't take the chance that the poacher would shoot her or Pablo, which meant Ben had to do something.

Fortunately, the gunman's attention was so focused on Vee and her flashlight flickering under his boat that he had not yet seen Pablo. He certainly hadn't seen Ben, running silently on the sand and almost at the boat.

He was calculating angles in his final approach to the speedboat. The tide had started to run; the first quarter of its six-hour cycle was its weakest, but out here on the cay, ocean currents came into play, and the stern of the speedboat was already being tugged by the outgoing water away from the anchor. The angle of the boat was working in Ben's favor. The gunman was looking forward, to the prow of the boat, where the light of Vee's flashlight bobbed about under the anchor chain. If he turned his head even slightly to the side, he'd see Ben.

But so far, he hadn't. So far, he hadn't noticed there was anyone else on the beach. Lucky, Ben thought. Then he noticed the light shining from the speedboat cabin, the tinny sound of music. Luck had nothing to do with it; the light and music playing in the boat cabin had masked their arrival.

He hoped like hell Pablo had thought to turn his own small flashlight off once he'd known there was a gunman on board the boat. He must only be seconds behind.

His breath heaved as he saw the gunman make a move. He was close enough to see the *huevero* was young, dressed in black and heavily tattooed down one arm. He looked tough, as though he'd been given his first gun in the cradle. He was making his way up to the front of the boat, gun arm raised towards the starboard prow, under which Vee was splashing about, oblivious to the man above her.

Three steps, thought Ben, his lungs at bursting point, his thighs on fire. He had to get to the man. He had to disarm him before he could have a chance to shoot. On the second step, he hit the water and the splash alerted the gunman. The man's head snapped around, and his arm started to follow. One step, Ben thought, and drove his body forward like a football player tackling an opponent. He heard the dull bark of the gun as his arms came around a shrieking Veronica and he dragged her down into the water, pushing with his feet to get them under the deepest section of the boat's hull.

His head broke the surface, as did Vee's, and he clamped his hands over her shoulders to steady her and haul her up with him so their cheeks brushed against the fiberglass of the hull.

"It's me, Veronica. Ben. Quiet."

A stream of creole invective flew over their heads, and he heard stamping about above them, followed by the broad beam of a strong searchlight flickering over the water at the prow of the boat. The man was searching the waterline.

He would shoot when he found them.

Ben could feel Veronica shaking under his hands. He put his mouth against her ear. "We have to disarm him."

She nodded.

He gave her a squeeze. "You have to make a noise at the front of the boat, distract him. Bang on the hull, anything. I'm going to climb up the outboard motor."

He felt Veronica shove something at him, as the rough waves under the boat buffeted them together. Something hard. He ran his fingers over it, recognizing its size and grooves. A galvanized shackle— shit. She must have disconnected the boat from its anchor. As soon as the boat drifted into deeper water, they'd be sitting ducks. He had to hurry.

A flashlight beam swooped near them, and Veronica sank beneath the water. He took a deep breath and did the same, feeling his way along the underside of the sleek speedboat until his outstretched arms felt the cold steel of the propellers. It was bruising work. The boat was slopping about in the choppy waters now that it was no longer anchored to the seabed, facing the wind. He braced himself for a second. It was now or never.

He wedged one foot into the shaft of the outboard leg and drove himself up from the water. The gunman was leaning over the front of the boat, but Ben's weight pulling on the motor had his head snapping round. His arm was coming up, the dull black of the gun in his hand almost invisible. Ben kept coming. He was over the transom now, leaping for the man's arm. His fingers just missed the gun, gripped the man's wrist, and his body weight slammed into the *huevero*. The thief was light, lighter than him by about twenty pounds, but wiry and strong.

He smashed the man's arm against the side of the boat, hoping to dislodge the gun, but he lacked power in his damaged shoulder. The man fought back, chopping at him in the neck, causing him to gag and lose his grip. His vision fractured.

With the shackle in his good hand, he made a fist around it, and drove it at the head of the *huevero*, hoping its added force would daze the man enough to loosen his grip on the gun. The gunman grunted as Ben's fist crunched into his nose, but they both started to slide in the saltwater that streamed off Ben's clothes onto the floor of the boat. They grappled for control, their bodies slamming into the vinyl seating, work crates over the floor cracking and splintering under their bodies as they fought.

He could hear Veronica screaming, then the booming shouts of Pablo, and the boat started to rock violently. The cool metal of the gun barrel was in his fingers, and he pulled it, trying to turn it, hauling the body of the *huevero* next to his so he could reach the handle. He almost had it, almost had control of the gun, when the gunman yelled something at him in creole and a crack sounded deep within his ears, deep within his chest, and his blood turned to fire and then as quickly to ice. He felt himself falling, stumbling to one knee. He clutched his chest, and his fingers found a slickness they did not recognize. Not seawater but blood. So much blood. He dropped like a stone to the floor.

Footsteps sounded about his head, but he barely heard them. A scuffle, a heavy thump, and then a flashlight was being shone in his face and Pablo was there, his wet face dripping down onto him.

"Ben. Ben!" Pablo's voice was frantic.

He tried to speak, but nothing came. He coughed

and felt the metal salt of blood in his mouth. He tried to breathe, but no breath came. He struggled to speak, just a word.

"Bullet."

Pablo was stripping off his own T-shirt, wringing it out, and pressing it into the part of Ben's chest that felt like it had been blasted by a missile made of ice.

"Veronica." Pablo's voice was deafening. "Put pressure on the wound. We have to go now, or we will not make the tide."

Veronica's frightened face swam into Ben's blurred vision. She was crying.

"I'm sorry, Ben. I'm so sorry."

She turned to Pablo. "How will we get him to our boat?"

Pablo's voice was the last thing he heard.

"We're taking this one."

22

*S*abrina sat with Maggie on the long bench in the shed. The volunteers who weren't out camping at the nest sites were up, roused by the news of the men ransacking the western cay.

Mickey had heard nothing on the FM radio since Pablo had called in to report they'd arrived at the cay. And that was over an hour ago.

"It can't be much longer, now," said Maggie, for perhaps the third time.

Tide charts were spread across the workbench. All the project workers knew how vital the tides were to getting the boat back over the reef.

It had been a tense hour. After the noise of the dinghy's motor had faded from the anchorage, Sabrina had left the *Silver Girl*, still too raw from her nightmare to settle. Too fragile from the night's emotional rollercoaster to think. She had hurried to the compound, where she had found Maggie in the kitchen wearing an apron and a worried expression.

"I like to cook," Maggie had said. "Especially when I'm flustered."

Sabrina pitched in with a batch of scones, as sure as Maggie was that the team would be keen for a predawn feast on their return.

The cooked scones were in the kitchen, wrapped in a tea towel, cold now after the long wait for the team's return.

Maggie checked her watch. "Radio them again, Mickey. Surely they're back in the boat."

"No problem," he said, pulling the transmitter out of its clip. "Pablo, this is Turtle Base. Do you copy, over?"

They all listened to the crackling silence.

"What's happening on the monitors?"

The girl at the other end of the bench pulled the earphones out of her ears and brought over the laptop she had been monitoring. "I've got a few different sensors working. We've got visual footage of the poachers, they're still at the nest site, around nest sixteen, but there's no sign that Pablo interrupted them. I've been listening, and there's not much to be heard above the wave noise, but you can definitely pick up some talking in Spanish. No shouts, no interference. I don't think Pablo was there at all. I've got visual footage of other nest sites around the island, but no movement there. I'm sorry, I have nothing to report other than that."

Maggie squeezed the girl's hand. "Thanks, Andy."

They all sat and looked at each other.

Mickey was the first to speak. "We know they got there. That's good news. It means the radio was working and the boat was working."

"Maybe the radio has had a malfunction on the way home," Andy said. "Why don't I take one of the walkie-talkies down to the dock? I can call you if I spot the boat coming in; the walkie-talkies can reach that far no problem."

Maggie nodded. "Andy, you're a sweetheart. Would you? I'd be so grateful."

"No problem."

The college girl slipped off the stool and headed down the track to the dock. One of the other students slid off the hammock where he was lying and headed off with her.

"Have you had poachers before?" said Sabrina.

Maggie grimaced. "Not here. Before we set up this project with the Anguilla National Trust, I worked on a project in Costa Rica where we had quite a bit of trouble." She smiled. "That's where I met Pablo, in fact. He was working as a ranger for the Ballena National Marine Park. I was bumming around the Caribbean with some girlfriends after university. I met Pablo, and that was that."

Sabrina pursed her lips. "You never went home?"

"Well, sure. Pablo was a huge hit in Dublin. Can you imagine? All that hair and Caribbean-Latino charisma trapped in a tiny Irish pub with my freckle-faced relatives? He had them under his spell in seconds."

"But what about your studies? What did you do at university?"

Maggie shook her head. "Interior design." She gave a laugh and glanced about the organized chaos of the work shed. "Not that you would think it. But I adjusted. Part of our role here is to raise awareness of our conservation work around the world. I picked up some pretty useful graphic design skills while I was at university, and I have an eye for color, design. So I look after our website, encourage the volunteers to blog about their time here, that sort of thing. Their social media networks extend pretty widely across the globe. It's great coverage for us."

Sabrina nodded. Maggie really had adapted herself into a new role. Different from the one she must have envisaged as a student, but building on the skills she already had.

"I couldn't have done any of it without Ben, of course."

She looked up. "Without Ben? Why's that?"

Maggie gave her a funny sort of half-smile. "Well. You know. The website, integrating all our data so I can share it with the sponsors. He set all of that up." She laughed. "Took him about half an hour to install it, then about two months to teach me how to use it."

"Oh. So he's a website designer?"

Maggie stared at her as though she'd grown a third eye. "Ben? You really don't know?"

"Know what?"

Maggie's next comment, whatever it was going to be, was lost in a flurry of chatter from the radio.

Mickey grabbed the mic, expecting to hear the boat radio, but it wasn't Pablo's voice he heard, it was Andy's on the walkie-talkie. He switched handsets and twisted the volume dial to its maximum.

"Andy? Can you repeat?"

"It's Pablo. He's here with Ben and Veronica but you need to bring the jalopy down to the beach. Right now."

The walkie-talkie screeched as though it had been dropped, then they all heard Pablo's voice, deep, urgent.

"Call a medivac helicopter. Ben's been shot. Tell them he's been shot in the chest."

Sabrina gripped the bench. The reactions of

Maggie and Mickey washed over her and reached the other students, who ran to the shed at Maggie's cry, but that faded into the background for her. Her chest had seized on a breath, and fear rippled through her like a curse.

This was her nightmare come true. It wasn't bitterly cold. It wasn't raining on the black cobblestones of inner-city London. But the call had come, and she would fail. Again.

She stretched her arms out before her and looked at her hands. Were they shaking? Her vision was so blurred, how could she tell? Her breath started to gallop, but then a sharp sound broke through her upswell of panic.

Mickey had pushed back from the bench and his stool flipped back, its metallic boom snapping at her inertia. He was running for the jalopy, parked under the trees on the side of the clearing.

Sabrina stood up.

She couldn't do this, but she had to.

She couldn't do this, but Ben might die if she didn't.

She couldn't do this, but she would.

"Wait," she said.

Her voice held the authority of fourteen years of training. Eight of them in the emergency department of a busy London hospital. Knife fights, bomb victims, acid victims, gun wounds: she'd seen and dealt with them all. Her voice cut through the rising panic in the compound and stopped Mickey in his tracks.

"I'm a surgeon. I'm coming with you."

She barely heard Maggie's cry of surprise, but looked at her steadily before she turned to run to the car. "Call that helicopter."

Thoughts crashed into her brain, thoughts of blood and grief, of lost opportunity, but she stonewalled them. She was a brain with skills. She was a trained pair of hands. That's all she could be at this moment. Not a person. Not a sister. Not a lover.

The ride to the beach took less than a minute through the rough sand track, the leaves of the trees snapping at their hair in the wild drive. The dock was ablaze with light when they reached it, its oil lanterns blazing. A group was huddled at the end of the dock, crowding over a still figure. Ben.

Sabrina ran up to them. She wanted to cry. She wanted to tell Ben she loved him. She wanted to explain to him that he was right to be suspicious about who she was. Because who was she? She didn't know the answer. She didn't have any answers.

"Have you called the helicopter?" Pablo's voice was hoarse. "He is unconscious. It's bad."

Sabrina fell to her knees. She could analyze her

feelings later, or ignore them, the way she had ignored her feelings for months. But now she had a job to do.

She put aside her indecision and let her brain and her hands take over. She spoke like one who expected to be obeyed. "Everyone, give me some space. Andy. Get me the first aid kit from the *Silver Girl*. It's in the galley, below the stove."

Her brain was taking in information, categorizing it, prioritizing it. The list stretched out ahead of her, one item after another. Face, pale. Too pale. Loss of blood, and no way to transfuse out here on the island. Blood from the mouth, and much, much more of it over his shirt.

She heard as though from a distance Mickey's words over her head. "Do as she says. She's a surgeon."

Ben's T-shirt was torn but still too tough for her to rip without scissors. There was no time to wait for the scissors from the medical kit. "Pablo. Rip the collar; I need his shirt open."

Pablo's large hands reached down beside her, and the fabric tore, its rasp loud in the predawn stillness.

And there it was. Holy-freaking-moley, she breathed to herself silently. Black blood, the consistency of molasses, wept from the wound. The hole was small, perhaps an inch across, and it was somewhere in the region of the sixth rib. But what was the angle of entry? What path had the bullet taken?

She held fingers to Ben's neck, counting, hoping for a healthier pulse than the one she was feeling. It was faint, too faint. He'd lost a lot of blood, and from the speckle of pink across his jawline, he'd punctured a lung.

He was alive, even though he didn't look like it. And he wouldn't be if that bullet had nicked his heart. He had to be stabilized, and fast.

Someone threw the medical kit on the dock beside her, and she flung it open, spreading its contents over the rough planks of the dock. Forceps, tweezers, bandages. Thank heavens, this was no glove box first aid kit. No doubt it was meant for emergencies offshore where no help was available. She held up a bag and read the label. Saline solution!

She looked up at Pablo. "How long until the helicopter comes?"

He looked uncertain. "It will depend on whether it's called out already. If we are lucky, ten, twenty minutes. If we are unlucky? I don't know."

"Where can it land?"

Tears ran freely down his cheeks. His shirt was gone, and Ben's blood matted the hairs on his chest and ran down his shorts. She could see the effort it was costing him to pull himself together. "The compound near the house is big enough. We can light a flare to guide it in."

"No," she said. "We can't move Ben that far. Can it land on the beach? Here?"

Pablo looked behind him, nodded. "It can be done."

Sabrina took stock. What she needed was instruments, lights, a team. Cameras and scalpels and a hygienic environment. What she had was a jetty, a beach, and competent but frightened spectators. She had to be in command.

"Mickey. Take the jalopy. Find out how far away that helicopter is and tell them the patient has a collapsed lung and needs surgery urgently. Tell them they'll be putting down on the beach. Then bring back flares, lanterns, whatever you need to make them land as close to us as possible."

"You got it." The boy ran off back to the car.

"Veronica?"

"Yes?"

"You're my assistant. You've got small hands, and you're good with fiddly electronics; you'll be best at handing me equipment. Pablo? Get the strongest flashlight you can find on Ben's boat. And a blanket. He's in shock, and we need him warmed up."

She lined up the equipment she would need in order: needle, tubing, saline sack. Scalpel, forceps, tweezers. Bandaging. Swabs. All of it was sealed, all of it was clean. Trust Ben to have such a thorough kit on board.

She doused her hands and Ben's chest liberally in disinfectant, then made Veronica hold her hands out and did the same to hers.

"Veronica, open the glove packet without touching the gloves, I need to get my hands into them without touching anything else."

It was tricky, but she'd had plenty of practice.

Getting the drip into Ben's arm was next. "Pablo, when I tell you, lift the saline bag and hold it steady. If we don't get some fluid into him, he's going to go into cardiac arrest."

She hovered over the vein with the large gauge needle; his pulse was so low it was hard to feel it in the back of his hand. She tapped until she was sure, then drove the needle into his arm. She pulled back on the syringe to be sure she had it, then fixed the tube into place.

"Tape," she said to Veronica. "No, the other one. Good." She bound the drip into his arm, and adjusted the drip rate to its maximum setting. It was the only bag she had; she was placing a lot of trust in that helicopter getting here pretty damn soon.

"Okay, now hold the flashlight steady, Pablo, as low as you can without getting in my way." She muttered a quick prayer to whatever gods might be listening over the Caribbean and eased the gauze back from the hole in Ben's chest. The bullet wound gaped there, horribly real. Horribly raw. She used the forceps to hold the wound open. In the beam of light, she saw a gleam of something. Metal—the dull steel of a spent bullet. And something else: the white splinter of broken bone.

"Okay. The rib's caught the bullet, which is good news. The bone has stopped the bullet from traveling deeper into the chest cavity. But where the rib's been hit, it's broken, and a piece of rib has punctured the lung. He's only got fifty percent lung capacity. It'll be the pain of the collapsed lung that knocked him out. The blood loss on top of that...well. He's critical."

"Is he going to die?" Veronica's voice was high, tearful.

Sabrina couldn't lie, even though she wanted to. "He might. He needs blood, and he needs his lung repaired with sutures, neither of which we can do here. But we can give him a fighting chance."

She counted to three in her head to steady her fingers, then reached into the hole in her lover's chest and gripped the bullet with the forceps. She'd done this before, plenty of times, but never without a full team of anesthetists and surgical nurses. Never to a man she had been with. She gave the bullet a tug and felt it move. She gave it another and wiggled it infinitesimally within the bone it had lodged itself in. The bullet was loosening its hold.

She eased her forceps open a fraction, took a new grip of the bullet, a deeper grip. "Okay, now," she whispered. "Come on, come on." And then she lifted the bullet clear of the wound.

A pink wetness surged from Ben's chest in the wake of the bullet, and she snapped at Veronica. "Swab. Now."

She rushed to pack the wound with the fresh gauze, then taped it into place with more packing before rocking back on her knees and looking up at Pablo and Veronica. "Where the hell is that helicopter?"

She reviewed what she had done. The saline bag was half gone, dripping steadily into Ben's arm. His face was slack. She probed his jugular again with her fingers, assessing his pulse rate. It wasn't better, but neither was it worse. She pulled the blanket up more securely around his chest, trying not to think about how recently she had smoothed her hand over that same chest with such a different purpose.

She felt a sob of reaction breaking through and rested her head briefly on his shoulder. "Come on, Ben," she whispered. "Hang in there, I'm begging you."

It was while she lay slumped there, her arms around him, that she heard the thumping of helicopter blades overhead. Headlights shone from the island track at virtually the same time; Mickey was driving the jalopy down the beach, using the head-lights to illuminate the beach end of the dock.

"Good boy, Mickey," she breathed.

She gripped Ben's hand in hers, her fingers clamped over his pulse. Lifting her eyes to the sky, she watched the helicopter land.

23

The smell woke Ben. Disinfectant. Bed sheets cleaned in some commercial machine a long way from the sun. Then the hum of air-conditioning made itself heard. It took him a while to connect his senses to his waking brain.

His hands rose to his chest. The icy fire...a gunshot wound! Memory dumped itself on him like a rogue wave: Sabrina, poachers on the island, rescuing Veronica from her mad scheme, leaping at a tattooed gunman. And then nothing.

He smiled dreamily and let his thoughts circle back to the start of it. To the important part: Sabrina. Who would have thought his Caribbean odyssey would bring someone like her into his life?

"Ben?"

His eyes snapped open. He knew that voice, but it

wasn't the one he wanted to hear. What in hell was his lawyer doing here?

He took a moment to look over his surroundings. He was in a hospital bed. The drab beige walls and overpowering whiff of clean were enough to tell him that. He was in a private room, and a bag of clear fluid was hanging on a metal scarecrow next to his pillow, dripping its contents into the apparatus strapped to his left arm.

He felt as weak as a kitten. He dragged a hand up to his face and winced. As hairy as a kitten, too. How long had he been out?

"How are you feeling?"

He let his gaze rest on the young man who was sitting on a chair by the side of the bed, a briefcase perched on his knees, looking pressed and primped to within an inch of his life in a pinstripe suit and a militarily severe haircut.

"Ned. You look like you're dressed for my funeral. What are you doing here?"

"Pablo called me. He's been here, day and night, but Maggie's gone into labor. He'll be with you when he can."

Ben frowned. "No one else?"

"If you mean Sabrina, then, no. She's not here."

He gave Ned a once-over. "You seem to be mightily well informed for someone who just got here."

Ned didn't even bother looking sheepish. "Well, that is why you pay me that handsome retainer."

He grunted. Where the hell was Sabrina? Another thought struck him. "Where the hell am I?"

"You're in the Margaret Mary Alacoque Hospital on Saint Martin. The medivac helicopter brought you here, then had to go back and collect Maggie, who'd gone into labor in all the commotion."

"And the poachers? Veronica? What happened."

Ned looked at his watch. "Pablo promised he'd make a wax doll out of me and stick me all over with paper clips if I didn't let him fill you in on all that's happened. He made me give him some hair. Don't worry, he comes by all the time. He'll be here soon."

Ben frowned. "He better be," he said, resting his head back into the pillows. Talking was exhausting. And he wasn't ready to even try and start thinking yet.

"So," said Ned after a pause.

He didn't bother to open his eyes. "So."

"I'm supposed to get the doctor if you wake up. You want me to get her?"

Ben felt like he could sleep for a week. "In a minute. Tell me what's happening with the restraint-of-trade case. I may as well get all the bad news out of the way in the one day."

"No bad news there, Ben. Your twelve months is officially up as of yesterday, and I was able to come to an arrangement with the hardass lawyer who was investigating you."

"What sort of arrangement?"

"A mutually beneficial one. I just pointed out to her what a waste of her time it was to continue to pursue you, when we all knew the case had no basis in fact and was just a money-grabbing exercise. I suggested she'd have a lot more success, and celebrity, if she devoted her talents to chasing some of the predatory practices of the real white-collar criminals."

Ben opened an eye. "I don't believe it. You offered her a job, didn't you?"

Ned allowed his usual poker face to slip into a grin. "She turned out to be an excellent investigator. My firm could use one. It was a win-win."

Ben yawned and felt the heavy wave of fatigue rise up over him. "Don't bother getting the doctor just yet," he said, and drifted back into an uneasy sleep. His legal problem might be dealt with, but that wasn't what troubled him. Where the hell was Sabrina?

THE NEXT TIME he opened his eyes, his room was bursting with people. Pablo sat on the end of his bed, a swaddled infant clasped gingerly against his massive chest. Maggie lay in the recliner chair in the corner, a grin the size of Christmas spread over her face. Veronica stood by the door, looking uncomfortable. A nurse was fussing about with his arm, pulling the threads of tubing out of the plastic apparatus attached to his wrist, and a ferocious-looking woman, who he assumed was his doctor, was standing at the foot of his bed, holding a fat chart.

He gave himself a moment to take in the faces, then let the nurse lean in behind him and rearrange the cushions behind his back.

Pablo reached to him and grabbed his hand. "Welcome back, my friend."

Ben gripped his, then let his eyes drop to the new arrival. "I see someone else decided to gate-crash my party."

Pablo's face was wreathed in smiles. "Little Bess. Meet your godfather." He spun the infant around so Ben could mutter something dutiful. She looked like a little chocolate dumpling wrapped in a pink blanket.

He leaned his head past Pablo's bulk. "Congratulations, Maggie. I'd kiss you if I could get up."

Maggie smiled roguishly. "I'd let you."

The doctor cleared her throat. "Right then, Mr. Ryan. Nice to make your acquaintance. You want me to get rid of all these people so we can talk?"

Ben looked around at the group. "No. They're

family; they can stay." He winked at Veronica. "You too, Vee."

"Okay. You've received a gunshot wound to the chest, entry occurring between the fifth and sixth ribs." She reached over to the side table and picked up a small plastic specimen jar. "Dr. Gray was good enough to keep it for us so we could make sure no fragments had split off."

He listened to her in silence. He had no memory of anything after hearing the gun go off and feeling his chest explode.

"The entry of the bullet was arrested in part by your rib, which stopped the bullet but broke. It was a broken section of rib which caused most of the damage, puncturing your lung."

Ben ran a hand over his chest, feeling the raised texture of bandage under the thin hospital gown.

"You also lost a lot of blood. Fortunately, Dr. Gray was able to get a saline drip rigged up and extract the bullet, both of which actions undoubtedly saved your life. You were very fortunate to have someone with such expert skills on hand."

Ben nodded. "Gotta love a medivac team."

The doctor pursed her lips. "No, you misunderstand me. Dr. Gray saved your life before the medivac team arrived. They would have been too late; the blood loss was too great."

He looked blankly at Pablo.

"Just listen to the doctor, Ben. I will fill you in soon."

The doctor made a few notes in her chart, then clipped it back into its folder at the end of the bed. "You will stay with us here for one week longer. Both your rib and your lung need to be monitored very carefully. The lung will repair itself quickly; the rib will take some weeks to heal. And after that?" She smiled for the first time since she began. "You will be as good as new." She gave him a brisk pat on the foot and left the room, taking the nurse with her.

Ben looked at Pablo, somehow knowing the answer even before he asked the question. "Dr. Gray took a bullet out of my chest before the helicopter arrived. Who the hell is Dr. Gray?"

His friend shrugged. "We were as amazed as you are now, Ben. But it is true. Your stowaway is a surgeon."

He felt stunned. He looked around at the three faces staring his way, feeling a wrench even more painful than the ice and fire of the bullet because of the fourth face he couldn't see. Eventually, he voiced the only thought that his mind could hold. "And where is my stowaway now?"

Maggie's voice was gentle. "I'm sorry, Ben. She's gone back to London."

IT WASN'T until many hours had passed that Ben felt ready to examine his thoughts about all that had occurred. A nurse had come by and helped him shower and shave, which had made him feel slightly less like a patient and more like a person. Veronica had come in to cry by his bedside for a while and apologize for being the cause of him being shot.

He had extracted the full story out of her of what had happened in those crowded hours before the dawn, after he'd been taken out by the gunman. How Pablo had climbed up onto the boat after Ben and knocked the gunman unconscious, tying him up with the ropes on board. Pablo's and Veronica's decision to steal the *hueveros'* speedboat and race the falling tide to leave the island. How Veronica's plan truly had contained glimmers of brilliance because the other *hueveros* were trapped and the authorities were able to round them up and take them into custody.

And then she had told him about Sabrina.

"She snapped into this badass leader. We couldn't believe it. Pablo was crying. Mickey was beside himself. Sabrina just took command. She made Mickey light up the beach for the helicopter to land. She wouldn't let Pablo move you up to the house. Pablo had to hold the flashlight, I had to open up the equipment—she raided your kit from the yacht—and she operated on you right there on the dock. It was like she was made of ice, I swear. When she took the forceps and shoved them into the hole in your chest? I would have fainted, but she was all "Get the swab now, Veronica" and "Six inches of tape, Veronica". We all stopped panicking. And then when the bullet was out and the drip was working and we heard the helicopter coming in, she sort of lost it for a bit and got all weepy, but then she started snapping out instructions for the paramedics and got into the chopper with you and flew off."

Ben had been silent, digesting all of this as Veronica spoke. "Was she here when you arrived?"

"No. By the time we got back to the compound, Maggie was starting to have contractions, so Pablo packed up Sabrina's gear, stuff for you and Maggie, and called another chopper to get him and Maggie to the hospital. I stayed behind to talk to the authorities and get the runabout back from the western cay. Mickey's in charge now, and Pablo's talked the National Trust into paying for a security guard to stay with the students while he's here. Everyone's pretty upset, as you can imagine."

Ben sent Veronica back to the Manatee Cays, helping her assuage her guilt by giving her a long list of chores to do on the *Silver Girl*. She skipped out of his hospital room looking like a kid who'd been given a truckload of candy.

But that left him here. On his own in a hospital room. Brooding.

He contemplated his laptop that someone had left on the bedside table, then pulled it over onto his knee and switched it on.

"Power up, Honey."

The machine clicked and whirred, and Honey's dulcet tones filled the room. "Only fifteen percent battery, Ben, darling."

It would be enough. He poised his fingers over the keyboard, and then he allowed himself to do what he never did: he used his skills to pull out every detail available, both publicly and privately, on Dr. Sabrina Gray.

24

*A*utumn had arrived in London while Sabrina was running away from herself in the Caribbean. The leaves along the cobbled walk in St James's Park were golden, and flurries of them rained down over the park in the chill wind.

She loved London. She loved its seasons, the snug pubs of winter, the long evenings of summer. Even the tourist crowds didn't bother her. She had grown up with them, grown up hearing their wonder at the history of the river, their delight in the changing of the guard at Buckingham Palace.

But for the first time ever, she had mixed feelings about returning. It was the right thing to do, she knew it was. She just hadn't expected it to be so hard.

She could have killed Ben. That was the truth that had finally broken through her trauma. She had to face that, and then she had to make her choice. She either accepted professional help, learned how to live with her feelings of guilt and grief about Cassandra without subsiding into panic, and then committed herself to her career, or she had to accept that her career as a surgeon was over. What she could never do again was operate on someone without being absolutely sure that her panic episodes were a thing of the past.

By operating on Ben before she had dealt with her trauma, she had risked his life. She could have had a panic attack at any time during that procedure.

It hadn't happened. She'd coped. He was stable when the paramedics loaded him up into the helicopter, and the surgeons at the hospital on Saint Martin had assured her he was out of danger. But when she'd sat by his bed in the recovery ward, where they'd allowed her to stay as a professional courtesy, and she'd seen his still form, the tubing keeping his lung inflated, the gray cast to his skin ... that was when she'd known she had to leave.

She had saved Ben, but only because luck had been on her side. And surgery was not about luck. It was about being sure. And she wasn't sure about anything, except the realization that the time had come to save herself.

Her mother had welcomed her back with open arms, thrilled that Sabrina was returning to see her psychologist, Dr. Ahnoud, and a-bubble with plans for the future, for Sabrina, for the Gray family.

"I'm thinking of a new fundraiser for the medical school, Sabrina. The Gray Bursary. What do you think? Awarded to a student in financial need."

She had let her mother carry on with her monologue of plans and glory. Her mother was who she was, and Sabrina was who she was. She should stop wishing her different, just learn to live with the mother she'd been given. It was just the two of them left now, after all.

She turned the corner into Victoria Street. This last session with Dr. Ahnoud had been liberating. She could feel the cloud starting to lift. Perhaps running away to the Caribbean had helped in some way. The student volunteers at the turtle project had been Cassie's age when she had died, and she hadn't thought of them as too young to make their own decisions. On the contrary. They were capable, adventurous, grown-up.

She had talked it out with Dr. Ahnoud, her guilt at not doing more to intervene in Cassie's life. Her worry that had she allowed Cassie's attempted theft of drugs from the hospital to be discovered, the police intervention may have saved her life.

"Your sister was an adult," Dr. Ahnoud had said. "You were not responsible for her choices."

And she was right. She was beginning to see that now.

With the approval of the board, she had agreed to return to the surgical lists the following week. She would assist for the time being, until she was sure her panic attacks would not recur with the sight of blood.

But for the first time in months, the cloud was starting to lift. For the first time in months, she was beginning to feel hope. She took a deep breath, taking in the crisp leafy breeze, the underlying brackishness of the Thames. Couples walked hand in hand along the pavement, leaning into each other, laughing over shared jokes. She dwelled, not for the first time, on that stolen night with Ben on the Silver Girl. It all felt so far away. So like a dream. He had broken through her defenses, made her laugh, made her feel. But Ben was half a world away, and her world was here, in London.

She'd nearly lost her career when Cassandra died, and without it, she'd been less than a person. She'd been living a shadow of a life, not a real one, and Ben was part of that shadow life. An unreal life where she was the sort of person who made up fictitious brothers, took desperate life-threatening risks when operating, and sailed away into strange waters with barely a thought for those she'd left behind.

But she was whole again now, or at least whole

enough. Enough to reclaim her career, reclaim her calm. She couldn't risk losing those again.

Her phone bleeped, and she stopped in her tracks to answer it. "No, Mother, I hadn't forgotten. Yes, I'll be there. Seven o'clock."

Damn. She had totally forgotten about her mother's ball. She pushed back the heavy woolen sleeve of her coat and checked the time. Four o'clock. She had some work to do if she was going to be dressed up enough to satisfy her mother by seven. Rebuilding her relationship with her mother was far from over, but she was trying.

Lifting a hand, she signaled a mini cab that was cruising past. Duty called.

Lady Gray had exceeded expectations, Sabrina thought as she walked up the staircase into her childhood home. The Georgian mansion blazed with light. Hired servers, clad in crisp black and white, gathered coats at the door, proffered silver trays of champagne and juice, and ushered guests through the hall into the heritage ballroom that dominated the rear of the house.

She handed her wrap to an usher, then took a moment to check her reflection in one of the mirrors that adorned the hall. She had owned the midnight velvet gown for some time, but hadn't found cause to wear it until now. It swept low across her décolletage, and the color matched her eyes. She wondered briefly if her mother would frown at her hair. She'd had no time to have it professionally styled, but had managed a passable job of a French twist. Her grand-mother's diamonds completed the ensemble. They looked like ice, she thought. Cold and hard.

Like her head needed to be if she was going to resume her career.

She frowned at herself in the mirror. The last touch of the Caribbean sun still colored her cheeks. When that was gone, she would truly be able to say goodbye to that chapter in her life. Perhaps then the pain in her heart would ease and she would be able to leave Ben where he belonged, safely in her dreams.

She nodded. She would do. She'd swan about as visibly as possible within her mother's line of sight and then disappear for an early night. A movie and a takeaway curry, perhaps. Or a book. Or she could catch up on her mounting pile of medical journals. All those options were a whole lot more appealing than prancing around at her mother's fundraising ball.

Squaring her shoulders, she walked to the arched entry of the ballroom and whispered her name to the announcer. Such an old-fashioned gimmick, she thought, as the dour-faced man in a plush Scottish kilt called out her name.

"Sabrina Gray."

Arched glass windows spanned the length of the ballroom, reflecting the glitter and glamour of the assembled guests. Chandeliers spilled their fractured light over the crowd, and massive ferns dotted the room. She saw her mother part from a cluster of people at the head of the room and turn to her.

"Sabrina, my darling. Only twenty minutes late."

Her mother floated towards her in a cloud of Dior, air-kissed her cheeks, and drew her hand under her arm. "I've found some lovely people for you to meet. Come with me."

Sabrina reached a hand out to a passing tray of glasses and snagged a champagne. She had the feeling she was going to need it.

Her heart wasn't here. Her heart was remembering the last party she'd attended, one where the guests were barefoot and the lighting ran on star power, not electricity.

"You know Maurice and Joan, of course, dear."

She plastered a social smile to her face, barely listening as her mother brought her up to stand with a group of guests.

"And their young friend." Her mother paused and leaned in so close to her that the scents of caviar and Krug threatened to overwhelm the French perfume. "Their young self-made billionaire friend," she added, softly, in Sabrina's ear. "Ben Ryan."

Sabrina's startled gaze hurried past the familiar faces of Maurice and Joan, her mother's particular friends, well-heeled patrons of many of London's fundraising societies. It skittered to her mother's beaming face, while she wondered, briefly, if she'd been hallucinating; if her mother had actually said two totally different words and she'd just warped them in her mind into the two words her heart wanted to hear.

But then her gaze landed on his face.

Her heart stuttered. Oh. It was Ben all right.

But it was a man far removed from the scruffy adventurer she'd lost her heart to among the Caribbean islands, even further removed from the pale and unmoving body she'd run away from in the Saint Martin hospital not twelve days ago.

He looked...well. Amazingly, jaw-droppingly, exquisitely well. His hair was cut, not a curl in sight, the blond locks shorn close, like a big-city banker. His cheeks were smooth, close-shaven, with none of the scruff she had run her fingers through, reveled in as it scraped along her breast.

She felt color rising up into her cheeks. She tried to speak, but words failed her. Her eyes roved over him. Surely he shouldn't be here? In England, four thousand miles from his hospital bed?

But here he most certainly was. He wore a tuxedo, in a dull coal black that emphasized his tan. He looked...thinner. But healthy. So much healthier than when she'd whispered goodbye, kissed his pale cheek.

Tears welled in her eyes. She held out a hand for him to shake, and he grasped it, warm fingers squeezing hers, fingers that she knew too well.

"Dr. Gray," he said, giving her the faintest quirk of an eyebrow.

"Ben, darling, call her Sabrina, please," said Lady Gray. "Why don't you show Ben the gallery, Sabrina. He's been expressing an interest in our quaint British customs."

With customary aplomb, her mother plucked the champagne from her hand and pushed them off in the direction of the stairs, away from the circle of people, leaving them, despite the crowded room, alone.

Sabrina felt numb. Ice-cold, in fact. The same temperature as the lump in her breast where her heart used to be. She felt confusion rushing back, uncertainties. She couldn't let them take hold. She had faltered on her path before, and it had nearly cost her everything she had worked towards, everything she needed to identify herself. She couldn't falter now.

Ben Ryan, the self-made billionaire. Her mother's words kept looping over and over in her head.

He gripped her arm. "Let's go to the gallery. I need to talk to you."

She set off for the private stairs that led from the ballroom through the hall and up to the gallery on the next floor, which housed a collection of art, family portraits mostly, of varying quality. The word *gallery* was a stretch of the imagination only her mother would use, but it would be quiet there. They wouldn't be interrupted. And she doubted Ben had traveled all this way to look at oil paintings.

25

They came to a stop near the curtained alcove of a large bay window overlooking the garden. Ben turned her, seizing her upper arms and holding her still. "God," he said. "Just let me look at you for a second."

She looked perfect. Like a princess in a fairy tale, her hair up in a complicated plait at the back of her head, earrings sparkling above that long, porcelain neck.

He slid his hand up her arm, over her shoulder, framed her face with it. He had so many questions, all of them urgent, so urgent he had flown around the world and inveigled his way into this party, but he couldn't help himself. He gave into the overriding urge to kiss her.

She gasped as his mouth came down hard on

hers, and he drank it in, drank it all in, pulling her velvet-clad body up against his, so that the swell of her pushed at his jacket, against the steady rhythm of his heart—the heart that she had stolen, then saved.

The back of her dress was low, crisscrossed with thin straps, and he let his fingers linger on the skin there, the coolness of it, the warmer patches where he skimmed his fingertips under the fabric, up the sides of her body.

She shivered, and he moved his head, lifting her chin, deepening the angle of his kiss. He wanted more. One night was never going to satisfy him, not a week, not a year.

She was making muted noises, urgent sounds, and he swiveled her around so she was pressed up against the ancient paneled timbers. He held her there, dimly aware of the gimlet-eyed ancestors frowning down at him. He leaned his forehead against hers, tried to catch his breath. Maybe the doctors back in Saint Martin hadn't been totally crazy when they said he shouldn't come. Since when had a hot-handed tryst left him so weak?

"Sabrina."

He stroked her hair, kissed her nose, gave her all the space he could to catch her breath, which wasn't much. His hips were nudged against hers; he could look down the front of her dress to the pale flesh beneath. "Tell me why you left."

She grew still beneath him, brought her hands up to push against his chest, then must have thought better of it. Who better than she would know of the still-healing wound there? She clasped his upper arms, pushed him firmly away, widened the gap between them until they were no longer touching.

"Ben. You shouldn't have come."

"What the hell do you mean?" He was having trouble reading her face.

"It was a fantasy, Ben. A holiday romance."

She didn't mean that. She *couldn't*.

Now that the joy of seeing her again had fizzed, he took his time studying her. Pale. Dark shadows hiding beneath a dusting of powder. There was something else at play here, and he was going to push until he discovered what. "I know about Cassandra."

"What?"

"I know the surgical board put you on probation after her death because you started having panic attacks in the OR. I know you've seen a psychologist because you no longer trust yourself. I know your mother's ambitious and you have nightmares in the dark, and I even know you've never had brothers who played rugby or dislocated their shoulders."

She stared up at him, open-mouthed, so he continued. "What I don't know, Sabrina, is why you would run away from me."

All the color had leached from her cheeks. "How do you know all this? Who told you?"

He held her gaze. "Not you, Sabrina. You didn't tell me anything about yourself. So I made it my business to find out."

"How?"

He shrugged. "The internet. It's all there, if you know how to look. And I know how to look."

She was turning away from him. "That stuff is private. Cassandra. My problems. It's private, Ben."

He was the angry one now. "Sabrina, you've had your fingers in my chest. How much more private can you get than that? You dug a bullet out of my rib."

He ran a hand over his heart, over the bandage that still prickled there. He sighed. "Not to mention the night we shared on the boat. Wasn't that private? For us both?"

She brought her eyes up to his, and her cheeks gleamed with tears.

"Sabrina." He softened his voice. He knew she'd been grieving, had been stuck in a spiral of anxiety that she hadn't been able to cope with. He was here to support her, not berate her. He picked up her hand, held it between his. He ran his fingertips over the shortness of hers, felt the practical length of her nails, the strength in her hands.

"I want to help you, if help is what you need. Hold your hand while you grieve. Be with you." He squeezed her fingers. "What I'm trying to tell you, Sabrina, is that..."

Crap, this was hard. If he'd ever spent a whimsical moment predicting the circumstances in which he'd be declaring himself, it hadn't involved tears. Or a gunshot wound. Or a clenched hand lying cold and inert in his.

He took a breath. He meant it, so he was going to say it, the circumstances be damned. "I love you, Sabrina."

Her head was shaking, and she wrenched her hand from his. "No. Don't say that."

"I just did. I love you."

"I'm not..."

He sagged against the ancient wall paneling and waited for her to finish.

She fixed her eyes on the buttons of his shirt. "I could have killed you, Ben."

He frowned. "You saved my life."

"I was lucky!" The sudden rise in her voice was enough to bring a waiter clattering up the stairs, and Sabrina turned her face to the window until the man passed.

Ben reached to touch her shoulder, but hesitated. "Help me understand," he said at last.

He could see the effort it took for her to square her shoulders and turn to face him. "I should never have thought I had the competence to take that bullet out of your chest."

"If you hadn't, I'd have died."

"Maybe. Maybe not. But if I'd *fumbled. Panicked...* you would have died on that dock with my fingers in your—"

She broke off and buried her face in her hands.

"Sabrina. Sweetheart. It's not your fault that I got shot. None of this is your fault."

She snapped at him, then. "You cloud my judgement, Ben!"

She repeated it, quietly. "My judgement. And without that, who am I? I'm nothing and no one. I'm not enough for anyone to love, especially you."

And she walked away from him, down the long corridor, down the stairs, and out into the night.

26

*W*eeks turned into months. Dr. Ahnoud closed Sabrina's file and sent her off into the freezing London winter with a smile and her best wishes.

The surgical board lifted the last of her restrictions, and she returned to her operations, busy, competent, in charge.

Her mother nitpicked her way through her choices, her wardrobe, her friends, but Sabrina felt calmer about ignoring her. She felt calmer about a lot of things, in fact. About everything except her heart.

She settled back into her routine. After all, this was what she'd wanted, hadn't she? This was what she had been protecting when she turned Ben away: her career, her identity, herself. Long days on shift passed. She spent her evenings sleeping or catching up with Antonia, whose love life was providing her close group of friends with its usual dose of drama. She flew to Hawaii for a girls' weekend to visit her friend Charlotte and tried not to look at the blue skies, the lush trees. The white yachts sailing on glittering seas.

The reality check, when it came, was from a source she would never have expected. Her mother cruised into her flat one December morning, a mink flung about her neck that would have driven the animal activists in the city into a frenzy. "Sabrina, darling. I've been thinking."

Sabrina paused in the act of pouring boiling water into a teapot and kept her tone light. "About what?" A party? The balding-but-aspiring-son-of-a-friend who she simply must meet? A committee she simply had to join?

"Cassandra."

She almost dropped the kettle. Her mother never brought up her sister. Ever. "Yes?"

"I know it's been difficult for you. Horrendous, in fact. Finding the body, feeling responsible."

Sabrina moved the teapot into the center of the table, dropped two lumps of sugar into her mother's cup. "Yes. It was brutal."

"The thing is, darling. I never had the courage to tell you. She rang me first."

She paused in the middle of filling her mother's cup. "First when? That night?"

Lady Gray nodded. "Perhaps an hour before. It was the usual phone call. She wanted money. She wanted to argue. No one cared about her." Her mother peeled her gloves from her fingers, readjusted her rings so they sat in line, their gems winking in the overhead light. "I brushed her off."

"Mum." She put her hand over hers. "Nothing you said or did made her take her own life."

Her mother pulled a miniscule but perfectly pressed handkerchief from her purse and dabbed it to her eyes. "I know that, Sabrina. But the same holds true for you. Nothing you said, or did or didn't do, made her take her own life. We had tried everything. We failed. In the end, it was Cassandra's choice to never learn from her mistakes."

Sabrina nodded. "I know that now. But it took me a long time to work it out."

Her mother patted her hand. "Here's something else you don't know."

She smiled at her mother. Advice, direction. She should have known it was coming. "And what's that?"

"Duty doesn't always come first."

This was not what she had been expecting. "Excuse me?"

"I've seen you. You work. You come home. But

there's more, Sabrina. Maybe it's time you took some of it for yourself."

She blinked.

"You've lost your spark, darling. Oh, I know, I've always pushed you. I've wanted things for you that weren't available to girls like me when I was growing up. But I never wanted you to miss out on life, Sabrina. I think, when you ran away to the Caribbean, I was upset, yes, but that was because I knew you needed to work through your grief here and not throw your career away over it. But you have your career now. And guess what? It is secure. You're an excellent surgeon, an excellent doctor. But you don't need to be using those skills here in London."

Her mother pulled out a compact, powdered her nose, then looked Sabrina right in the eye. "I've been wondering if maybe it was time you ran off to the Caribbean again."

She couldn't believe this was her mother speaking. "But you've given your life to St. Joseph's hospital. I always thought you wanted me to work there more than anything."

Lady Gray finished her cup of tea and took her time sliding her manicured fingers back into her gloves. "Perhaps I'd like to see you living life even more. We won't know until you try. See the world, Sabrina. Find your own place in it."

She sat for many hours thinking after her mother

had left, and her last words kept revolving around in Sabrina's head. *See the world. Find your own place in it.*

Find her own place.

She almost didn't know how to start thinking about what her own place would look like. She just knew who she'd like to see standing in it.

S abrina was just in time to witness the last of the clutches hatching. She stood in the moon-dappled shallows, shining her flashlight down on the furiously paddling baby turtles. They looked like polka dots against the white sand.

"I never get over the thrill of seeing them swim to safety," said Veronica.

Sabrina smiled. "You know the statistics better than anyone, you've been rattling them off to me for hours. Fish nets, sharks, exposure. How many will make it out there in the ocean? They're not swimming to safety, not really."

Veronica stood next to her, her colored bandanna rippling in the onshore breeze. "Nothing is ever one hundred percent safe, is it? Where would the adventure be, if it was? Perhaps that's what I find so thrilling. They're swimming out there towards life, hope, a future."

Sabrina was silent. The baby turtles weren't the

only ones who were taking a plunge into deep water tonight. She had been back on the Manatee Cays for three days now, taking a crash course on turtle conversation while she waited.

For every minute of those three days, she'd hoped to see the tall mast of the *Silver Girl* rounding the breakers of the channel through the reef. Working with the volunteers, learning to salsa with Pablo under the mauby bark trees, even swinging in the hammock with Little Bess hadn't been able to quell the tension of the wait.

Pablo and Maggie were expecting Ben. Their daughter was due to be christened on the island, and Ben was the guest of honor. They hadn't seen him in a few months. He'd been in San Francisco doing a contract for a government who needed a bank saved or their nuclear arsenal protected, according to Maggie. Sabrina wasn't entirely sure if she was joking.

And tonight, as she had set off with Veronica for the late shift supervising the last of the unhatched nests, she'd seen the unmistakable lights of a yacht coming into the dock.

Ben was here.

Veronica clearly knew where her thoughts had drifted. "Have you seen him? You know, since the shooting?"

Sabrina flicked a look at the younger woman. "Briefly. It didn't go well."

"Why? What did you do?"

"I pushed him away."

Veronica began walking up the beach, gathering the clipboards and cameras, her spade, the bucket of gadgets she lugged about everywhere. "I reckon he'll forgive you. He forgave me for getting him shot."

Sabrina watched the last of the baby turtles disappear through the waves, where the beam of light from her flashlight didn't penetrate. Forgiveness had been at the heart of her anxiety for the past year, her own inability to forgive herself for not being able to save Cassie. But then, Cassie had not been alive to say the words, as Ben had been able to say them to Veronica.

Cassie's ability to forgive her, or blame her, had died with her that wintry night. And so, she'd had to learn to forgive herself. It had just taken a long time for her to do it.

She turned and followed Veronica up the beach to the jalopy, helped her load their gear. "I hope you're right," she said.

The dock was quiet when she reached it. It was past midnight; life was busy here on the island, and all the residents were tucked up in their tents. Even Little Bess had seemed content to sleep through the night as Sabrina tiptoed through the house at the end of her shift.

The sky was ablaze with stars, ribbons of them, as though painted with a light-dipped brush. She'd not taken the time to learn the names of the constellations; she'd been too caught up pursuing her studies, keeping her feet moving along the path she'd laid out for herself. But she'd learned over the last few months that only looking straight ahead was no way to navigate through life.

Now she was ready to look up. To look around. To live like the adventurers of old, setting sail from the known with the wind at their backs, and hope in their hearts. Like sea turtles, she thought, smiling at her newfound knowledge. Putting their trust into the warm currents of the ocean and the map of stars they carried in their ancient genes.

A soft waft of tropic breeze lifted the hair on the nape of her neck, pushed her blouse against her back. She felt it coax her onward, down the dock, and so she walked forward, the wind at her back.

A golden shaft of light was coming from the aft cabin of the *Silver Girl*. She ran nervous hands down her shorts, smoothed the loose braid in her hair. The box step wasn't in its usual place. Ben had arrived late, after dark. Perhaps he hadn't wanted to disturb the family up at the house. She put a hand around a stainless-steel stanchion and hauled her way up on board the boat.

Ropes were coiled, sails were stowed. Everything gleamed in the soft light of the full moon. The hatch down to the saloon was open, and she headed down it, her bare feet making no noise on the timber steps.

The familiar, blinking lights of the chart table lit the saloon with flashes of amber and green. Ben's laptop was propped open, its screen dark. Sabrina stopped as a thought struck her. Perhaps walking in on Ben in his private cabin was too much of an assumption. An even more horrid thought struck her. Perhaps he wasn't alone?

She ran her hands over her face, sucked in a breath, then made her mind up. He had come all the way to England to find her. Now it was her turn to be courageous. To take a chance. Turning to the chart table, she trailed a finger over the mousepad of the laptop and watched the screen spring to life. She typed a random sequence of letters into the password box and waited for Ben's watchdog, Honey, to respond.

She wasn't disappointed.

"Ben, darling, someone is trying to break into your computer."

The words boomed from speaker to speaker about the boat, then faded into a silence broken only by the faint whir of a motor deep within the cabinets of the galley, the soft lap of water against the hull of the yacht.

And then a sound.

A brush of knuckle, perhaps, against the varnished paneling of the cabin. The slap of bare feet against hardwood floors.

And then the cabin door opened, and Ben was standing there in the doorway, a halo of golden light from the lamp behind him throwing his face into shadow. His chest was bare, a sarong hooked low about his hips, and a rumpled paperback novel dangled from his hand.

It was too much. Just too damn much to see him there, in the stillness of the night, the sight of him an echo of the last time she had been on the *Silver Girl*. Of the few hours they'd shared in that cabin before he had zoomed off in a battered old dinghy to get shot. Before she had left.

Surprising herself, she started to cry.

"Sabrina?"

She tried to speak, but it seemed now the tears had started, they didn't want to stop.

"Sabrina."

She felt his nearness a second before he touched her, felt the rumpled-bed warmth radiating from him. A large hand closed on her shoulder, his other arm pulled her in to his chest, and she rested there, her damp cheek against him, listening to the steady thump of his heart.

When she could, she raised her head, eased herself away. She needed to apologize. She needed to explain, and she could do none of those things while weeping on his chest.

She met his eyes, not sure what to expect. It had been months since she'd seen him on the evening of her mother's ball, when she'd barely given him time to speak before pushing him away.

He gave her a long look, his face difficult to read. "What are you doing here?"

She took a deep breath, and the carefully rehearsed words of apology, of explanation, evaporated from her thoughts like dewfall under a hot sun. All she could think about was their last night, here, on the boat, together.

"Do you remember once you said to me I might have some questions of my own to ask you?"

Ben scratched his jaw; she could hear the faint rasp of bristles under his fingertips. "You've flown four thousand miles to ask me some questions?"

She nodded. "I have. So many questions. But first I need to explain."

She took in a shaky breath. It felt like she was about to perform open-heart surgery, but on herself. "I'm a little nervous. Do you think I could make us a cup of tea?"

"I'll make it. Why don't you go sit up in the cockpit; it's cooler up there. I'll bring it up."

It was peaceful on deck. The dark was lit only by starlight, and the moon was streaked by thin wisps of cloud. She could feel the peace soaking in, feel her own readiness to accept it. She had her life back. The sorrows and blame and anxiety were gone. Dealt with. Only, her life felt different now. The rigid course she had set for herself was no longer exerting its pull, and she was glad of it.

A thump from the stairs brought her head around. Ben was there, a tray in his hand, which he placed on the table. He settled into the upholstered seat opposite her.

"Green tea okay? It was that or beer."

"Green's great," she said, her eye on the lopsided owl tea cozy he had plunked onto the teapot.

He saw her looking at it. "It was Maggie's idea," he said, and poured the tea out into two heavy-bottomed mugs. "I've been teaching her how to manage the Turtle Project's blog, and she wanted to pay me, but you know..." He smiled sheepishly. "I don't want to take her cash. So she suggested a trade. Skill for skill."

"And you chose knitting."

Sweet. There was no other word for it. If she hadn't already known she was mad about him, she would have fallen for him there and then. She accepted the cup he handed her, took a sip. The silence built about them, and Ben let it stretch out, didn't press her to begin. At last she was ready, and it all came pouring out. Growing up with a sister who challenged every rule, a mother who valued ambition, a father who died before she could really know him as a person. All she knew of him was his reputation, his triumphs, his successes. She never knew if he had doubts. If he liked sugar in his tea or ate popcorn at the movies or cheated at scrabble. He was an icon, not a person, and her mother encouraged her to worship him. And the more Sabrina followed in her father's footsteps, the more the distance grew between her and Cassandra.

And then Cassie took her own life.

"I was too late. The police were there, paramedics, but she'd cut her arms too deeply, too well. And seeing all that blood—"

She paused, gulped at the hot tea, grateful when Ben moved his hand and placed it over her own.

"I'm sorry."

She nodded. "That's when I had my first panic attack. And they didn't stop. I could no longer deal with blood, which meant I could no longer work. My mother reacted like both her daughters had died: the troubled one by suicide and the good one by throwing away her career. And so, I ran away."

Ben's fingers were making little curled patterns

on the palm of her hand, like the inner whorls of a shell.

"To the Caribbean."

"I know, it's such a cliché, isn't it? But running away didn't help. It didn't matter where I was, what bed I was waking up in, all I could see were my own problems, my own worries, repeating over and over with no end. And then I woke up in a bunk on the *Silver Girl*."

Ben's eyebrow rose. "In my T-shirt."

Sabrina felt a leap in her pulse rate. She cleared her throat. "And you didn't know who I was. Which made two of us, because by then I could no longer remember who I was, not really."

She broke off, stared over the quiet waters of the bay to the fringing reef, where she could hear the ocean breaking over the exposed coral.

"And something happened, Ben. I can't explain it. The ocean. You. Sailing. I felt happy."

He gave her hand a squeeze. "You don't have to explain that to me. I get it. What I don't get is why you couldn't tell me what you were going through."

She sighed. "Because if I started talking about my fears, I'd have to acknowledge what they were. And I wasn't ready to do that. And then you were shot."

Ben's other hand moved to the scar on his chest. "And you saved my life."

"Yes." Sabrina smiled. "Thank god. But at the

time, all I could think was that I could have ended your life. I was in no condition to be performing surgery. And so, I ran away again. That was when I hit rock bottom. So I did what my mother had been urging me to do for months. I returned to the psychologist I had been seeing. Dr. Ahnoud helped me acknowledge my fears: that maybe I would never work as a surgeon again, and that in my dreams, maybe my sister would always blame me for letting her die. And when I started to acknowledge them, that's when I started to heal."

"And now? How do you feel now?"

"New. Hopeful. Nervous."

"Nervous about what?"

"About what's going to happen when I tell you why I'm here."

Under the table she felt a warm foot come to rest against hers. He squeezed her hand. "Why don't you give it a go?"

She didn't give herself time to think, or to plan; she just said it. "I love you."

Ben swept the tea tray to the far side of the table. He grinned and hauled on her hand. "Well, thank heaven for that, Sabrina. Come closer and tell me again."

She scooted around the bench seating, and he hauled her onto his knee. "I was so afraid you'd be over me."

He pressed his cheek to hers, held her there. "I can't tell you hǫw close I came to coming back to London. I would have, too, if your friend hadn't sent me the odd email, let me know how you were going."

She reared her head back. "My friend? What friend?"

"Antonia."

"That rat."

He grinned. "Mmm."

"But you've never even met her."

"Well, that's not strictly true. When you left me at the ball, I was leaving when she arrived. Your mother introduced us, and when I said I was going to crawl into the nearest bar and get rat-faced drunk on whiskey, Antonia volunteered to come with me. She had man trouble."

"She always has man trouble."

"So we swapped sob stories and cried in each other's drinks, and by the end of the night, she had my email address written on a five-pound note and I had made a vow to break the legs of a pilot called Tyler if ever I had the misfortune to find myself on a plane with the loathsome heartbreaker."

She laughed, feeling her anxieties peeling away. "Poor Antonia. I'll miss her."

"Uh-huh?"

He didn't sound like he was listening. He'd turned his attention to her hair and was pulling its hair-tie away from the bottom of her braid, threading his fingers through the long strands so they fell around her shoulders.

"I quit my job."

"Great." His voice was muffled, his face pressed into the soft skin beneath her ear.

"I made a few calls. I can work out here easily, in the islands with ties to the Commonwealth. Less easily in the States, but it's doable."

His mouth was on her neck in an open-mouthed kiss that was messing with her ability to think.

"I just thought, you know, we could take some time to get to know each other. I could work near you. See how this goes. If you want to."

He was working his way upwards, his lips feathering a path to hers. "I might have an opening for a pancake cook."

She smiled, pulled her face away an inch or so when he would have claimed her mouth. "I'm serious, Ben. And besides. I only do crepes."

"We can work wherever you like. Here. London. Timbuktu. Just so long as you don't leave me again. Now stop talking, will you? I'm trying to kiss you."

So she let him.

THE CLEARING around the house was decorated with palm fronds and colorful flowers. Pablo's family were visiting from Puerto Rico, and Maggie's family were visiting from Dublin, vastly outnumbering the handful of college students living at the Turtle Project. There was enough food on the tables to feed all of them for a month.

Mickey was back again for another season. He was in the hammock with the baby, letting her blow noisy bubbles into his harmonica. Veronica was rigging up party lights in the trees. Everyone else was dancing.

"So, after Little Bess's christening, I'm thinking of heading back out to sea."

Sabrina spun out from Ben's hand in the salsa move Pablo had taught her, then spun back in to rest, breathless, against his chest.

She smiled. "Oh really? Just before dawn, I suppose."

"I like to be out at sea for the sunrise. That way, when the trade winds blow, my sails will be up. I'll be ready to go with the wind."

He held both her hands as they moved with the music, their bare feet ruffling the broad-leaved grass in the clearing. She could feel the length of him from knee to breast. It wasn't enough. She didn't think she would ever get enough. She leaned up, pressed her cheek to his close-shaven one, murmured in his ear.

"Hmm. So if a desperado on the run was looking to hitch a ride, where would the dinghy be?" Her eyes were shut, but she felt his cheek crease as he grinned.

"Well, it's currently up on its davits. But I'll tell you a secret."

She moved her hand, held in his, so it was between them, pressed to her heart and to his. "Tell me."

"I never lock the boat."

She smiled. "How very risky. You might end up with a stowaway one day."

He dipped her then, low over his arm, pressed a kiss to the exposed column of her throat.

"I'm counting on it."

Loved this book?

Read Antonia and Tyler's story *HERE or visit my website*

Read Charlotte and Jack's prequel story *HERE* (free for subscribers to Stella's newsletter) or visit my website

Turn the page for more ...

ISLAND FLING

*A*ntonia pulled her new jaffa-red suitcase from the carousel, teetering on her heels as the full weight of the case nearly knocked her over.

"What have you packed in that thing, Toni?" said Charlotte.

She gave her friend a grin. "I was panic packing, so I can't really remember. Random outfits, umpteen pairs of shoes, a polka dot bikini. I've never been to a wedding on an isolated coral cay before. I wasn't sure what the dress code would be."

"Mmm. You sure you haven't tucked a few pounds of work in there too?"

Antonia turned for the customs gate, pushing away the thought of her problems at the office. She'd spent the flight out working, so now she was taking a break from worry until Monday when she flew back

260 OF STELLA QUINN

to London. "A girl's got to eat, Charlotte. You want a hand with anything?"

Her friend smiled and rested a hand on the barely-a-bump baby belly that curved the front of her dress. "I'm fine. Jack turned into an overprotective mother hen the day I told him we were expecting again. If we deny him the pleasure of carrying my bags, we'll ruin his day."

Antonia slung her hand through her friend's arm. "You're a lucky girl," she said, her eyes resting on Charlotte's husband as he expertly wrangled two suitcases, a tote bag of toys and a fractious toddler into an orderly line.

"It was good of you to organize a charter flight from Ballena to the wedding, Jack," she said. "Thanks for including me."

Jack perched his son on his shoulders and gathered his wife into his free arm. "No problem. The thought of two planes, an island taxi, and a wet speedboat ride with a toddler in tow was making me lose my hair. Chartering a sea plane to the Manatee Cays was an entirely selfish gesture on my behalf, I can assure you."

Antonia grinned. There was enough hair on Jack's handsome head to rethatch the British princes. "Your sacrifice is duly noted."

The Manatee Cays. Just the name of it sounded romantic. She sighed, just a little, and wondered why a reunion with her old schoolfriends, Charlotte and Sabrina, should feel so bittersweet.

She adored her friends, she did, but marriage had changed their friendship, even though they'd sworn a pact it wouldn't. She could accept it, because she could see how happy they were. Charlotte had been the first to leave the sisterhood, and this afternoon, after Sabrina tied the knot with Ben on a scrap of sand in the Caribbean ocean, she'd be the only one still single.

Antonia Da Silva, spinster. *Spinster!* Whoever invented that hideous-sounding word should be sent into a dungeon and cursed.

She sighed. Her friends hadn't even been looking for love, and they'd stumbled across it. Not like her: she'd devoted her adult life—and much of her adolescent life, too, if she was honest—to the pursuit of romance and adventure, and where had it got her?

As a teenager, she'd dreamed of being swept off her feet, carried away to exotic locations, being feted and adored by some tough-jawed, soft-eyed prince charming. She'd long ago abandoned those silly notions. Mostly. And she didn't need to be swept off her feet to be carried away: she could run on her own two feet towards adventure. In stilettos, if she had to.

But for some reason, romance and adventure had proved elusive. All of the princes she'd found had developed warts, like a wife, or an on-again, off-again ex-girlfriend, or commitment issues.

She handed her passport over to the customs official and followed the Diamond family out into the glare of the airfield.

Ballena. She breathed in the salt and humidity. Her plane from London had arrived over three hours ago, but she'd not stepped outside the terminal yet. Waiting for Charlotte and her family to arrive from Hawaii, typing out a few urgent emails for work, spritzing her way through the perfumes for sale in duty-free—she'd been too busy to take stock of the view through the airport windows.

But here outside the airport terminal, it all came flooding back. Perhaps that was why she was feeling a little blue. It had been in Ballena, after all, that she'd had one of her failed romances.

She still bore the scars from that one—they were crisscrossed over her heart, the way she'd crisscross a manuscript when she was editing it. Only, when she was at work, editing the articles published in *Bella Magazine*, her marks improved the article. She was yet to work out how the marks left on her heart had improved her. On the contrary: some of the wounds to her heart felt like they'd never heal.

"Auntie Toto."

She felt a fat little hand tugging at her skirt,

smiled, and swung Charlotte's little boy up into her arms.

"Yes, my precious pumpkin?" She'd long since given up trying to teach Charlie how to say Auntie Antonia. She was fine with Auntie Toto.

"Charlie likes planes."

She smacked a kiss into his plump cheek, making him squeal. "Do you, Charlie? What about sea planes?"

The little boy looked around. "I see lots of planes, Auntie Toto."

She chuckled. "No, my lamb. We're going on a special sort of plane today, called a seaplane. Look, there it is, can you see it?" She pointed across the glaring concrete of the runway towards a neat little blue-and-yellow plane.

"I can see it."

"It's called a seaplane because it can land on water. That's what's taking us to Manatee Cays today."

The little boy slung his arms around her neck. "Charlie likes seaplanes," he said.

"Me too."

At least, she hoped she did. She'd never actually been on a seaplane before.

A baggage attendant had pulled ahead of them in a vehicle that looked a bit like a golf buggy and was towing their luggage in a metal cage. Charlie was entertaining himself admiring his reflection in the mirrored lenses of her sunglasses, so she didn't take much notice of the man in the pilot's uniform until she'd reached the airplane's tiny staircase.

But she noticed his voice.

"Jack Diamond," she heard Jack say, as he reached out a hand to shake the pilot's. "Thanks for meeting us here."

"You're very welcome. Four passengers, the booking says; so we're all here?"

That voice. Antonia peeled one of Charlie's hands away from her face so she could see for herself what her ears were refusing to believe.

The pilot wore whites: white shorts, a white short-sleeved shirt with epaulettes and stars that she barely processed because her eyes were skittering up to his face.

A pilot's cap was pulled low over his forehead, and his eyes were shielded by sunglasses. But that hint of dark hair shadowing his jaw...that flash of grin as he welcomed Jack and held Charlotte's arm to assist her up the narrow stairway into the tiny confines of the seaplane's cabin...

And then it was her turn.

Music was playing from the inside of the plane, a tinny little waft of Caribbean reggae that drifted down the stairwell alongside the smells of air conditioning and musty carpet. She had a sudden vision of herself, a flashback, looking up as she was looking up now, into the same face. But the time she remembered was three years ago, when her heart was still free of scars and she'd felt as happy and carefree as this music.

The pilot hadn't recognized her yet. His attention was still directed towards Jack and Charlotte as he pointed them to the tiny seats that furnished the interior of the plane.

But then his hand found the crook of her arm, and he was smiling as he turned to help her up the stairway.

"Watch your head as you step into the plane, ma'am, it's a low—"

She watched the smile drop from his face, and felt a teensy—okay, massive—amount of satisfaction as his jaw dropped slightly.

So. Maybe the rat hadn't totally forgotten her.

She hoisted Charlie around to her other hip and removed his fingers from her bottom lip, where he was busy trying to smudge her lipstick all over her face. "Captain Cooper. We meet again."

"Antonia."

He didn't sound overly thrilled to see her. Well, that made two of them; she wasn't overly thrilled to see him, despite the giddy somersaults her heart was flipping in her chest. She wouldn't have thought it possible to find a better-looking guy than the Tyler

Cooper of three years ago, but the living proof of it was standing before her. Three years had barely touched him; if anything, his jawline was more chiseled, his mouth even more delectable than—

She dragged her thoughts off his mouth and reminded herself that this was the guy who'd brought to a smashing end the most intense two weeks of her life. She'd been blissfully surfing the wild wave of romance and adventure she'd found in his company, and he'd wrecked it all.

She decided to swan past him as though she'd moved so far beyond him he was barely a recollection and mounted the stairs into the plane.

Jack took Charlie from her and buckled him into his seat, and Antonia moved through the tiny aisle. Charlotte gave her the googly-eyed look of interrogation.

"Captain Cooper? Were you reading his name tag, or do you know the guy?"

Antonia frowned at her. *Later*, she mouthed. She kept frowning as the captain entered the plane, pulled up the stairway after him, and made his way to the cockpit. What had he called their relationship, when he'd carved those scars into her heart?

Just an island fling.

TYLER FLICKED through the start-up procedure of his Cessna and tried to concentrate on the voice from the control tower talking in his ear. Every second word seemed to be Antonia.

Flight Alpha Yankee Antonia, you are cleared for Antonia...

He was losing it. "Control tower, this is Alpha Yankee 6446. Repeat clearance, over."

"Flight Alpha Yankee 6446, you are cleared for takeoff."

"Copy that."

Tyler took a second to shut down his emotions. He was good at that—he needed to be. Flying needed a cool head, and no one's head was cooler than his.

He flipped the switch on the intercom in the passenger cabin. "We've been cleared for takeoff. Please make sure your seatbelts are fastened. If you've not been in an amphibious plane before, you might find the takeoff a little steep. Nothing to worry about; we'll level out pretty quickly, and you'll be able to enjoy the journey over to the Manatee Cays."

There. The social part of the charter flight was over. He flicked a glance into the mirror that gave him a wide-angle view down through the cabin, then wished he hadn't. The copper-bright hair of the little boy shone in a shaft of sunlight coming in through the cabin window, and in the seat behind him, gazing over the airstrip, was Antonia. Those eyes—like honey melted through dark, sweet rum and her smile—as warm as it was generous. He felt a stab of pain, deep in the part of his soul that he'd locked firmly shut. His Antonia: the English girl he'd lost his heart to, back when he'd thought his heart was his to give.

Mind on the job, Tyler.

He grimaced. Even he was referring to himself by that name now. He couldn't remember the last time he'd been called by his real name. Shoving the thought aside, he pressed his finger to the ignition and watched the propeller sputter and then catch, its revolutions causing the body of the plane to judder against the brakes.

He used the flaps to guide the plane out through the apron markers and onto the runway, before clamping the brakes on. His hand tightened over the throttle—a hand that had once held the woman sitting barely eight feet behind him—and the plane's propellers ripped through the resolutions, faster and faster, until the fuselage rocked with leashed power. He felt the same urgent desire to yield, to release the brakes he'd had to clamp down over his own life the day he'd had to run.

He swore under his breath. He could never yield. Never.

Slipping the brake, he allowed the plane to surge

forward on the runway, feeling that release of tension he always felt with a joystick under his hand, and wings spread out to either side of him. The world below fell away, and the seaplane climbed, a push of power and ingenuity and cold-molded steel, up into the sky.

God, he loved flying.

He banked sharply to clear the congested airspace above Ballena International Airport, not unhappy to be leaving. Ballena served as a transport hub in the Caribbean. International flights serviced it daily, and tourists used it as a gateway port for the many smaller islands in the Caribbean—too many tourists.

He'd made money there, sure, back before he was spotted three years ago. Recognized by a dumbass minion from the drug cartel in the States, who knew his real name and his former occupation. He'd had to switch his base of operations to St Novia after that near miss. Kept his visits there short.

He could never rest easy, because one day, someone else would recognize him. He could never get involved with a woman, because they'd get caught up in the shitstorm that was his past life. He found his eyes traveling to the mirror once more— and his gaze locked with Antonia's.

Her hair was longer, its golden-brown curls clustering about her head like an angel's. A fallen angel, he thought, as a memory pierced him: wild days and wilder nights, from that crazy, idealistic, foolish two weeks they'd spent together back...when? When he'd been on the run so long, he'd forgotten how to be cautious.

Well, he'd learned his lesson.

There'd be no more trysts for him with beautiful women whose skin skimmed like parachute silk under his work-roughened hands. whose laugh could cut through his worries into the warmth he'd forgotten he possessed. The risk for the women was too great.

His eyes dropped to the little boy again. He'd made the right decision. Antonia had clearly moved on with her life. The two-foot-tall living proof of it was sitting in his wing-side seat and galloping a plastic dinosaur along the arm rest.

He hoped she was happy, even while a little part of him hoped she could never be as happy as she'd been when she was with him.

An accented woman's voice began speaking in his ear, and he acknowledged the message from the control tower. He was out of Ballena air space. Next stop, the Manatee Cays in Anguilla.

He switched the plane over to autopilot and pulled his clipboard out of his flight case. Paperwork was a necessary evil for any pilot, and his more than most, seeing as he was the boss and owner of this plane and half a dozen others. Island Escape Aviation was the only thing he cared about. The only thing he *could* care about.

A sqwark from his watch some time later let him know it was time to start paying attention. The whale-shaped mass of Anguilla was looming below them through the light cloud. He switched on the microphone that connected him to the cabin.

"Hi, everyone. We're just traveling up the east coast of Anguilla. Soon we'll be able to see the Manatee Cays come into view. There are two of them; we'll be landing in the lagoon of the larger cay, where we'll be able to motor over to the jetty and see everybody and their luggage disembarked without having to get their feet wet."

He dropped his eyes to the clipboard as he spoke, checking his flight plans for the next day. "I'll be returning to the cay tomorrow morning in time to collect you all at ten o'clock."

He flicked the microphone into the off position and checked his watch. About thirty minutes from now he'd be back in the air, making the short hop over to Saint Martin for a cargo flight. He nodded; two birds with one stone. He'd earn money from a charter to help him pay down his big-as-hell business bank loan, and he'd put a few hundred sea miles between him and the girl currently sitting in seat 2A on his plane.

It was a win-win.

His plan went belly-up on landing. Well, not quite belly-up, but it was enough to turn a few hairs grey, even on a seasoned pilot like him.

The problem was that Manatee Cays wasn't a designated seaplane port. It was barely a designated boat port. Why anyone would plan a wedding there, and expect guests to be able to make it, was more than Tyler could comprehend.

The only people who lived on the island were the staff and volunteers of a turtle conservation project, and they didn't fly in—they came over from the big island in a speed boat. None of them had thought to do a sweep of the lagoon for floating debris.

Tyler brought the plane down in a low swoop over the lagoon, angling his wings so he had the longest stretch of protected water for landing. He eased back on the throttle, skimming just feet above the waves pounding on the outer fringing reef. He felt the skids kiss the water and bounce, just a little. He eased the joystick back a fraction more, and the skids bit into the water, slowing them down into a nice easy glide.

"Piece of cake," he muttered, then bit off an oath as the bleached white back of a submerged log rolled under his port float. His hands tightened on the controls, and he hauled on the joystick, willing his speed to be enough to lift them clear of the danger. *A log!* Heaven only knew what other obstacles had slipped over the reef edge on a high tide.

They could have skimmed over it. They would have skimmed over it, but for a swell of wave moving across the lagoon which brought the end of the log up just as his port float passed over it, and then all hell broke loose.

The sea plane canted into a hard turn to left, and the crash and bang from behind him let him know his passengers' luggage and toys and handbags had just scattered from one end of the cabin to the other. He fought with the controls to keep the nose up, revving the engine to keep enough lift so the port wing didn't stab into the water.

That would be a disaster, and Tyler wasn't having a disaster today.

"Come on, girl," he muttered, and suddenly, the wing lifted and he was clear. He brought the sea plane to a sharp and shuddering stop in the calm of the lagoon, but rather than risk sinking at the jetty, he decided to motor in to the sand. Until he'd been out there and seen for himself, he didn't want to guess at what damage the log may have done to his float.

He pulled off his earphones and the cacophony from the cabin nearly ruptured his eardrums. The kid was crying, and three adult voices were making a valiant effort to calm him down.

"Charlie doesn't like sea planes," he heard the little man wail.

Tyler blew out a breath. If he was wailing like that, he hadn't been injured in the rough landing. He flicked the switch on the microphone.

"Rough landing, sorry, folks. The plane float hit a submerged log. I'm going to bring us up onto the beach in case the float's taking in water. There's nothing to be alarmed about." Nothing for the passengers, at least. A ruptured float was going to seriously stuff up his own plan to take off before he could fall under Antonia's spell again.

When he'd nudged the nose in to the beach, Tyler let the plane stairs flop open and made his way down them to where cool sea water lapped over his leather loafers. He sighed. They'd been wet before; they'd be wet again. He glanced at the float, at the gash running along the length behind the wheel hub. Wet shoes weren't the biggest problem he'd be facing today.

The lady with the auburn hair was the first to the door, with Jack's face peering round behind her. "My wife's pregnant. I'm sure she's fine—she assures me she's as tough as old boots—but if you could help her to the shore?"

Tyler swept her into his arms and carried her the few steps necessary to find dry sand. He set her on her feet. "You sure you're okay?"

She smiled at him. "I'm fine, Captain. Great job on a tricky landing."

The little boy was next, wide-eyed and wail-free. "We're at the beach, Daddy," he was saying, as Jack passed him to Tyler, who stood, arms outstretched, ready to receive the toddler.

Daddy? But that meant—

He shook his head. It didn't matter what it meant. He was the charter pilot today, nothing more. A pilot who had no business wondering whether his ex-lover did or did not have a copper-haired son.

Jack had made his own way down the stairs by the time Tyler made it back to the plane, and he lifted the luggage hatch for him.

"Thanks, pal."

"No problem."

Which just left Antonia. She stood on the sea plane steps, her silver heels slung in one hand, her sunglasses back on her face. The breeze over the water whipped at her dress, billowing it about her lean curves in ways that made him forget his promises to himself, the restrictions under which he had to live his life.

He held out his hand, and she raised her eyebrow at him. Then, after a second, she took it. Her warm fingers clasped his own, and it was as though the years between them vanished.

He could have let her wade to shore. Hell, her

shoes were already off. But the devil in him made him cast caution to the sea breeze. He tugged her hand, swept his arm beneath her knees so she fell on his chest, her body bumping warmly into his.

It took just four strides to walk her to the beach, but it was four strides too long. He felt his heart break one more time.

TROPIC STORM

CHAPTER ONE ... A SNEAK PEAK

*C*harlotte Jones paused amid the crowded departure lounge of Los Angeles International Airport. Shining up at her from the display rack at the front of an airport shop was the familiar cover of *Bella* magazine. But was it the latest issue?

She broke into a grin as she pulled the glossy magazine out of its stand. Her last article had made the cover; she hadn't expected that. A dancer slumped on a backstage prop, all heels and legs and bling, her oversize feathers discarded on the floor beside her. Charlotte ran a finger over the dancer's weary face, the loud pop of color from the flamingo pink of the feather. The photographer had nailed it this time.

"You buying that, lady? You wanna library, you're gonna have to go someplace else."

"Relax, I'm buying," she said and placed the magazine down on the counter. She'd have a copy waiting for her when she returned home to London, stuffed into her mailbox and wrapped in a yard of biodegradable plastic, but why wait? She'd never gotten over the thrill of seeing her freelance articles in print, and she had a six-hour flight ahead of her. She'd be able to read the magazine cover to cover.

"A bottle of water too, thanks."

She rifled through the pound notes in her purse until she found her clip of American money, then handed a ten-dollar bill to the rumpled man at the till. Leaving the change on the counter, she headed back into the flow of people and cast a look upward to the screens. The letters clicked over on a departure board, white font over a black background: *Hawaiian Airlines to Honolulu, terminal 5, gate 58.*

A thrum of anticipation joined the jitters in her chest. This was more than a holiday about to start; this was a one-woman retreat, just for her, a journey towards peace, solitude, well-being. She crossed her fingers, pinkie-promised herself that it would work. As much as she loved her job writing opinion pieces in magazines and her hobby-slash-obsession writing for her women's issues blog, she needed to recover before going on assignment again. She closed her eyes and imagined the sunshine, saltwater, and sea breezes soothing her jangled nerves. Hawaii and happiness...she couldn't wait.

The queue to enter the waiting lounge at her gate was snaking down the corridor by the time she made her way through the sprawling airport. Couples leaned on each other, taking selfies to pass the time, and children squealed and bounced with excitement. An elderly woman wearing pearls the size of mothballs was having a heated discussion with a check-in attendant about the size of her carry-on luggage.

Charlotte smiled. People, chatter, hustle and bustle: she'd forgotten how much she used to enjoy the chaos of travel. And today, despite the crowds, she felt good. She felt strong, for the first time in months. Perhaps her psychologist was right and she really would recover. There'd been days when she'd wondered if she'd be trapped by stress forever. How would she work then?

A tinny voice from overhead broke her train of thought. Just as well; now was not the time to be dwelling on what had happened to her in Barwick three months ago.

Passengers on flight HA4 to Honolulu, your plane has been delayed. Please remain near the departure gate and await further instruction.

A collective groan issued from the people queued about her, and she shuffled forward with them through the security check. She'd spent a lot of time in airport lounges over the years. What was an hour or two more?

She slung her leather carryall on to the conveyor belt, showed her passport and ticket to the check-in attendant, and was waved through to the dubious comfort of the holding area. At least there were seats available. She chose a plastic chair by the window and settled in to wait, rolling her shoulders to relax some of the kinks. It had been a long flight over from London, and she was tired.

A toddler nearby broke into a wail, breaking her train of thought. Flashing a look over to the departure screen to check how long she was going to be trapped in a seat next to a young person with lungs the size of Texas, her gaze fell on a dark-suited figure entering the lounge, and all thoughts of kinked muscles fled from her brain.

"Oh my," she muttered.

A handsome man was walking through the security screening area. She studied him covertly over her magazine. Six foot one, she decided, skimming the length of him from his close-cropped, dark-blond hair to his expensively shod feet. His suit was the darkest gray, emphasizing the white of his collar and cuffs, and the body it covered left Charlotte's lips forming an *oh* of admiration. She wondered what color his eyes were, then turned resolutely to her magazine.

She'd never been lucky where men were concerned, no matter what their eye color, so really, what was the point in looking? She flipped through the glossy pages to her article. *Bella* had been her first serious job, back when she'd thought being an investigative reporter in war-torn countries would be a great way to prove to the world that she had made something of herself. Luckily for her, she'd been to school for a time with the magazine's news editor. Antonia still contracted her for the odd article, which helped keep the funds flowing in. And this latest one had been a delight to write. It wasn't her usual piece —she was more at home advising women on ways to hop, skip, and jump over the gender pay gap, or reviewing the latest mindfulness apps bombarding the market—but something about the chorus girls in London's latest stage show had appealed to her. The hard graft behind the glamour, the sweat beneath the sequins...she had found something when she interviewed the dancers which had resonated. The drive to succeed came at a price. For the dancers, it was the injuries, the uncertainty of work ahead, the competition for work within a shrinking industry.

Charlotte knew about paying a price for success. She'd spent the last decade paying it.

The toddler's wail reached a pitch capable of shattering bulletproof glass, and she cast a glance about, wondering if it would be too obvious if she changed seats. Oh, yes! There was one free, and—oh, happy day—it was right next to Mr. Hot Suit. She glanced up at his face, only to encounter him looking back at her with shocked recognition. Oh my god. No, it couldn't be. She dropped her eyes to the magazine she held in her hand and felt heat rushing up through her cheeks.

Jack.

The calm she had been feeling, the happy puff of anticipation about starting her holiday, evaporated. Her hands gripped the *Bella* issue as though it was a shield. Why did it have to be Jack?

She peeled her fingers off the magazine, noting how clammy her palms had become. She had to calm the hell down. Finding herself in the same departure lounge as the man who had smashed her world to smithereens nine years ago...it was too much. Maybe she could have dealt with it calmly if she wasn't already a mess about the fiasco in Barwick. But the fiasco had happened, and she was all out of bravery.

She kept her eyes averted, knowing she was behaving like a big chicken, but unable to help herself. Hopefully, he'd have the decency to stay well away from her. She did not know if she could handle a confrontation with the man she had once been foolish enough to lose her heart to.

Ladies and gentlemen, a voice blared from the speaker above her head, *we are pleased to announce flight HA4 to Honolulu is now ready for boarding.*

Oh, thank heaven. The airline companies fit three hundred people on these planes; with luck, they'd be seated well away from each other. She had an eye mask in her bag and ear plugs. She'd wrap an airline blanket around her head if she had to. She could not face Jack. Not now, not ever.

She slung her bag over her shoulder, checking her belongings were all safely tucked away, then rose to her feet. She marched to the boarding gate, checked her pass, then took off down the long airbridge to the plane. Fast walking was *not* running. Charlotte Jones did *not* run away.

"Well, not often," she admitted to herself as she sank into the plush comfort of her seat. She closed her eyes and willed her heartbeat to settle into a calmer cadence.

Her phone buzzed, and she reached to silence it. The words *Antonia is calling* scrolled over the glass screen. She sighed. Antonia wasn't just the editor of *Bella* magazine—she'd have ended the call if she was, future work prospects be damned—Antonia was also one of her oldest friends and was not the sort of person you could ignore, even from half a world away.

She lifted the phone to her ear and braced herself for the onslaught.

"Charlotte, have you arrived? Tell me everything. Is the water warm? Are the cocktails cold? Wait. Any single guys? You know I've got weeks of holiday owing; I can be there like a shot if there's single guys."

Nothing changed. She smiled. "Toni, I'm nowhere near Hawaii. I'm parked on a tarmac in the States. No cocktail umbrellas in sight."

"Bummer. Call me the instant you get to the hotel, won't you? I'll worry if you don't."

"Yes, matron."

"None of that cheek from you, young lady. But seriously, how are you coping with the crowds? No dramas in the airports? No panicky whatsits?"

She closed her eyes, and a vision of the gray-suited drama called Jack came into view. "Not that sort of drama, no."

There was a pause. Charlotte imagined her friend's brain scrambling through the innuendo of that remark. She chuckled to herself at Toni's next words.

"Tell. Me. Everything."

She let out a breath. Was she ready to talk about

it? She sighed and took the plunge. "You'll never guess the man I just saw at LAX."

"Umm. A Hemsworth? Hugh Grant? Colin Firth?"

"Somebody I actually know."

There was a pause. "I'm struggling here, Charlotte. You live like a nun. Do you even know any men? I can't think of a single one you've given tuppence about since Jack bloody Diamond back when you were a cadet journalist in London and I was backpacking my way through the single men of Europe."

The silence stretched out as Charlotte waited for the penny to drop. Or tuppence, in this case.

"Holy crap. You're not seriously telling me you ran into Jack Diamond?"

"Yep. The rat himself."

"I'm speechless."

Charlotte laughed. "Well, that's a first."

"So, what happened?"

"I ran away."

"Ran away? You? Charlotte the badass women-are-champions blogging queen?"

She could hardly believe it herself. But the heart was a tender thing, and she'd forgotten how tender hers could feel. "It was actually pretty tough seeing him, Toni."

She could hear her friend's nails tapping on a

hard surface. Antonia was at work, no doubt ripping adverbs from some hapless reporter's article.

"Yeah, I bet," Antonia said at last. "Listen, Charlotte, I have to take a call from Barcelona, but we should talk this out. Oh, and you know that draft article you gave me? The one on the Barwick riots?"

Oh yeah, she knew that one all right. She'd written it up in her hospital bed while under the influence of a surfeit of common-sense-dulling drugs. Well, she hadn't so much written it as dictated it into her phone, as her arm had been buried within six inches of plaster. Thousands of words on the women's issues blogger who'd been on her way to a café to interview a woman about a community gardening project but instead found herself in the middle of a riot that swept through the regional city when police shot a man in the street.

She regretted having written it now. She'd been too raw, too deeply affected to be objective in her reporting. Antonia could delete it; that was fine. "Don't worry about the article, I shouldn't have sent it in."

"Don't worry about it? Girlfriend, it is fantastic. I've entered it into the press awards. It's taking center stage in the next issue of *Bella*."

"Antonia—" She drifted to a close. Thinking about that day still had the power to upset her. She'd not be reading the article when it was published.

She heard her friend sigh down her end of the phone. "Charlotte. We don't have to talk about this now; forget I mentioned it, okay? Why don't you skype me when you're settled in Hawaii? I'll invite Sabrina over to my place, and the three of us can bitch about men and bossy editors until you get that sad little sound out of your voice. I don't like hearing it."

Charlotte smiled. Bossy or not, Antonia was as fabulous as a friend could be. "It's a date. And thanks."

She slipped her phone over into airplane mode and dropped it into her bag. She was lucky to have Antonia and Sabrina in her life, and she knew it. Her old school chums had been there for her through the high moments and the low.

The muted hubbub of the filling plane was comfortingly familiar. She turned to her window and gazed across the vacant seat through to the busy airstrip. Only a few more hours until her holiday started. The website for the hotel she had booked promised perfection. Part of the Jewel Resort Group, the Jewel of Oahu was set amid lush Hawaiian gardens, with views spanning a perfect beach and the Pacific Ocean beyond.

She sank into a daydream of bathing in sun-dappled water and lying in the feathered shade of coconut palms. She could think about the project her psychologist had been encouraging her to pursue or maybe read the half dozen books she had included in her luggage. She smiled. Would she read the rom-com first? Or the new thriller that—

"Excuse me."

Charlotte opened her eyes and sat up, reaching out an instinctive hand to smooth her wayward auburn hair. Oh, no. Fate couldn't be so cruel.

"If you wouldn't mind letting me past so I can get to my seat," Jack said.

"Of course," she muttered, rising to her feet. And she'd better get her wits together while she was at it.

She stepped out into the aisle of the plane, her gaze locked on to his. He was even more impressive than she remembered. Her breath caught, and she felt a surge of heat travel through her until even her fingertips tingled. She pressed herself against the seat on the other side of the aisle to widen the gap between the man who had broken her heart and her afflicted senses.

Jack stowed his briefcase and brushed past her in the narrow confines of the airplane corridor. His suit coat dragged at the linen of her dress, and she breathed in his scent, a clean, warm smell overlaid with a whisper of cologne. She gripped her fingers into the worn fabric of the plane seat and forced herself to look away. Any view would be preferable to watching Jack slide past her just inches away.

She waited a beat, then risked a glance sideways.

Jack was seated. She could do this. She could blank him out for the next few hours the way she'd been blanking him out for the last decade. Schooling her features into a neutral expression, she sank once more into her seat, giving him a cool nod.

He raised an eyebrow and held out his hand. "It's been a long time," he said. His American accent reminded her of their differences.

"Has it?" She wanted very badly to ignore that outstretched hand, but pride had her reaching out to shake it. Why give him the satisfaction of learning how flustered she was?

His warm hand closed briefly around hers. Memories of those long fingers and how they felt against her skin crashed through her thoughts. Blanking him out for the last decade hadn't been enough; she should have tried harder. Hypnotism. Therapy. Exorcism. She was saved from having to indulge in further conversation by the arrival of an in-flight steward bearing a tray of drinks.

"We haven't seen you for a while, Mr. Diamond," said the steward.

Jack helped himself to a glass of water. "Work's been keeping me in the States lately, Graeme. How's life in the skies treating you?"

First-name basis with the cabin crew? Jack must be a regular on the flight to Honolulu. She had forgotten he had grown up there. Well, not so much *forgotten* as forced herself to forget. She helped herself to a glass of champagne and nodded her thanks to the steward. Jetlag, fatigue, lack of sleep... her travel was catching up with her, and she took a large sip to steady her jangling nerves. How on earth was she going to survive the next six hours?

If only he'd grown bald and smelly. Or was traveling with a plump wife and screaming toddler triplets in tow and had carrot puree mushed into the front of his suit. Her eyes shot a look over to his left hand before she could prevent them. No ring. Not that she cared. But still, there was no denying it, he was better looking now than the day she had last seen him, when he'd leapt into a taxi and taken off to Heathrow Airport and left her outraged and crying on the curb.

How gullible she had been. How utterly, stupidly foolish to think he had been any different from her parents, from the world. Charlotte closed her eyes against the sting of unshed tears. She would not let this man know how much she still hurt. Pride was all that had kept her going after Jack sauntered out of her life. Her pride and her career. She was damned if she would be losing that too, after all this time.

She could barely remember the girl she had been. An idealist, a dreamer, all enthusiasm and passion and no wisdom. How ironic: she, who'd vowed to forge a career from words and make her living investigating the deeper truths of an issue, had just crawled into a hole of misery when Jack left. She'd not hunted him down and forced him to return. She'd not beaten a path to his door and wedged herself there until he'd explained why a big-buck salary on the far side of the world was more important than her. She'd been too hurt.

Too young, she acknowledged.

She was not that young, foolish girl now. If she weren't feeling so vulnerable after the incident in Barwick, maybe this could have been an opportunity to question the ghosts of her past and finally let them rest. But she *was* vulnerable. This time, she had to put herself first, which meant the last thing she needed was to complicate her much-needed holiday. She would find out where he was headed so she could avoid any further accidental meetings.

Fueling her courage with the last inch of her champagne, she laid a hand on the arm of his chair.

STELLA QUINN'S BOOKS
ROMANCE | ADVENTURE | ESCAPE

What readers have said

"X-factor nailed it. You can start bidding wars with this."

"I want to buy the trilogy – actually, I want you as my new best friend."

"Wonderful voice and loved your humor."

"Really enjoyed these characters."

The Island Escape Series
- can be read in any order -

Romance and drama on sun-dazzled beaches - the heroines are fun and the heroes are heart-throbs, why not escape with them on your own vacation romance?

Prequel novella: And I Always Will (Charlotte & Jack)

Book 1: Tropic Storm (Charlotte & Jack)
Book 2: Stowaway (Sabrina & Ben)
Book 3: Island Fling (Antonia & Tyler)
Christmas novella: Catching Snow (Lisa & Ryan)

The Clementine Springs Series

Small town romance set in Upstate New York - horses and steamboats, country music stars and lakes, why not head escape the crisp mountain air and discover love again?

Spring novella: The Umbrella Diaries (Marianne & Duncan)
Christmas novella: All I Want (Prudence & Adam)
Book 1: *Summer Loving* (Leila & Damon)

Other Books

Keeping Katie: A Gold Coast Retrievers story (Sweet Promise Press)

Australian Rural Romance

The Vet from Snowy River (Harlequin MIRA)
Heartwarming small-town romance

A New Ending (a novella set in Western Qld - FREE for subscribers)

Finding Home (a short story set in the Flinders Ranges)
The Cockatoo Track (a short story set in the Northern Territory)
Looking Back (a short story set in Qld)

To chat, and hear about new releases and library visits, and all things Stella, why not join my reader team! www.stellaquinnauthor.com/subscribe

For books without links here, head on over to my webpage for up-to-date information: www.stellaquinnauthor.com